Race of Hearts

The **Full Circle** Series

SHARON CLARE

Vickie,

May you always have love in your life.

Sharon Clare

RACE OF HEARTS

Cover design: Book Nook Designs.
www.sharonclare.com/book-nook-designs/
Cover Art: Deposit Photos, www.depositphotos.com

RACE OF HEARTS/Sharon Clare—First Edition
ISBN-13: 978-1975768249
ISBN-10: 1975768248

FREE BOOK FOR YOU!

Want to learn more about Sharon's books and receive FREE exclusive content? Join Sharon's email list on her website at: www.sharonclare.com and get a free book!

For my son Michael (who may cringe at having a romance novel dedicated to him.) You couldn't be a better son.

RACE OF HEARTS

Thirteen years ago, Adair Ellis told a little lie. A lie with big consequences for high school heartthrob Josh Symington, a guy who never knew Adair existed. Adair vowed no more lies, never again, but when she and Josh meet in Race of Hearts, a competitive singles event, she becomes the queen of deceit.

As they compete against other couples in romantic challenges, the unrequited crush she had on Josh in high school comes back with a vengeance. And this time, the passion is mutual.

She'll do anything to keep the past buried, even if it tears her apart along the way. But someone knows what she did and that someone thinks she should pay.

CHAPTER ONE

Adair Ellis wasn't convinced that sharing a secret she'd kept for thirteen years was a good idea. No better an idea than wearing a turtleneck in spring. She fanned herself with her notepad. Considering there'd been snow on the ground a week ago, the temperature in Stonewood Hill's community centre was unseasonably warm. Or maybe it was her.

"Some of you are carrying guilt," said Annalise, facilitator of Full Circle's emotional well-being group. "Allow yourself to feel it, pay attention to what it's telling you, and then you can let it go."

Good grief, she read me as if I have self-reproach stamped on my forehead.

Adair pushed her sleeves up to her elbows. Many of the fifteen women sitting in the circle looked sombre, but it was anyone's guess if guilt dragged them down. She only knew what sickened her own insides.

She looked back to Annalise. Friendly, intuitive eyes were framed by elegant cat-eye glasses under an auburn blunt cut. In cage heels, camel pants and abstract floral blouse, Annalise had the kind of good fashion sense that endorsed her credibility and a knack to sound both authoritative and accepting.

"I hope you all found the homework useful," Annalise said. "It's important to be aware of any negative beliefs you've carried forward from the past, so they don't poison your future. Before we finish for the day, would someone like to share the letter they wrote to their teenage self?"

Sitting to her right, Adair's friend Jessie gave a nudge and whispered, "Here's your chance."

Adair shook her head, suddenly filled with uncertainty.

"You said I wasn't to let you weasel out of this."

The vise around Adair's insides squeezed tighter. Her secret seemed to cry: *don't expose me. I like it here festering in the dark.*

But that wasn't helpful. She'd joined these sessions because this secret kept her awake at night.

Just do it—tell the truth.

Adair swallowed and raised her hand. "I'll share mine. I found the exercise useful, it helped me see things differently."

"Oh? How so, Adair?" asked Annalise.

"Well, surprisingly, as I wrote the letter, I felt compassion for the girl I used to be, the girl who felt inadequate, klutzy, unloved, and like you mentioned, full of bone-crushing guilt."

"I'm glad you looked back with compassion. Emotions are never more difficult to manage than through the teenage years. Would you like to share the cause of that guilt, and then we'll do some work to release those feelings."

Adair crossed one leg over the other, glancing down at her grey, ruffled skirt. She flipped the page on the notebook in her lap, but didn't read from her letter. "I did a terrible thing in my last year of high school, something selfish I still feel guilty about."

"We all did stupid things in high school," said Cassidy, a thrill-seeking chef.

"I hope so," said Adair. "I mean that in a misery-loves-company kind of way."

Annalise leaned forward in her chair. "It can help to look back and revisit what happened. Sometimes the stories we've been telling ourselves are not reality, so it's important that you don't judge yourself."

"I had a terrible crush on this guy Josh," Adair said. "It was obsessive and inappropriate since he was another girl's boyfriend, Carly. Carly admitted she only dated him because he was the star quarterback and good grief, he was hot. He was in my art class, but didn't know I existed. I thought Carly didn't deserve him, so I fabricated a story that broke them up. Josh took the break-up pretty hard and drove his car into a wall."

A woman sitting beside Annalise spurted coffee from her mouth and began to cough, drawing everyone's attention.

"Lydia, are you okay?" Annalise handed her a napkin.

The silver-blonde nodded and continued to cough into her hand. "I'm sorry, excuse me. I—I . . . it went down the wrong way. I'm fine." Lydia's face had gone from pink to pale, but she waved her hand in front of her tear-stained cheeks motioning Adair to continue.

Adair waited a few more seconds to be sure Lydia was okay. A shudder turned her cold as images flooded her mind, images of how his hopelessness must have looked. She'd often wondered how desperate a person would be to end his life in a violent crash like that. "Josh survived, but he never returned to school. I was devastated when I learned what he'd done. I ruined his life because of my obsession."

"You couldn't have foreseen a reaction like that," said Giselle, an energetic yoga instructor, and then the group of women erupted with platitudes.

"If you want to let go of that guilt, you have to feel it," said Annalise, a few minutes later. "When it comes up, pay attention to it, but don't judge it, don't fear it. It's just a feeling. Allow it to happen. The more you resist, the more it will try to get your attention. Acknowledging the feeling, allows you to let it go."

By the time the meeting concluded, Adair realized that sharing her worse secret hadn't caused hellfire to rain brimstone, and the guilt inside her had diminished a lot.

Women began to pull on their jackets and say goodbye.

"Adair, don't ever think you don't deserve to be loved," Annalise said, unexpectedly.

"Of course not. I don't think that." Did she? No, she'd made a break-through today. No more thinking about Josh. No more guilt. No more lies. No more secrets. "I know a wonderful man is out there for me."

Lydia, the woman who'd choked on her coffee earlier, approached Adair. "Thank you for sharing your story. Your words so touched me that I'd like to offer you a free ticket to an elite event. It's a dating race, if you're game. There's a $25,000 prize."

As Adair took the ticket, she noted the mess Lydia had made of her nails—turquoise polish scraped off three fingers.

Adair read the ticket. "Race of Hearts, a Cushion Club event. This ticket is $175.00. I can't accept such an expensive gift."

"No, I insist. Please, you'd be helping me out. I'm on the organizing committee, and I promised to recruit players, but I got behind and ran out of time."

"I've never heard of the Cushion Club."

"It's an upscale club that provides dating services and match-making events. They have a beautiful resort with a pool, spa and golf course. Race of Hearts is like a small scale Amazing Race geared for romance. For the competition, you'll be partnered with a potential love mate based on your personality, values and life goals, so be sure to fill out the questionnaire on the website to activate your ticket."

"Romance, huh."

"Oh, yes. The tasks you'll complete are meant to heat things up. Check the website. It explains everything." Lydia touched Adair's shoulder. "It'll be great fun. Something a little different, and there's a good chance you'll find the man of your dreams and get everything you deserve."

CHAPTER TWO

Josh Cohen cursed under his breath as he peered around a display of dog toys in Big Pete's Pet store.

Fourteen-year old Paige Duncan didn't see him watching her. She was focused on the puppy she slipped into her backpack. After closing the zipper, she carefully picked up the bag and held it to her chest. When she headed down an adjacent aisle, Josh quickly backtracked and caught her before she reached the end.

"Hey, Paige, how are you doing?" Planting himself in front of her, he crossed his arms over his chest.

The color drained from her face. "J-Josh. What are you doing here?"

"Your mom called me. She said you and her had a pretty bad argument, and you took off."

She groaned. "So she called my social worker. Are you supposed to work on Saturday? Don't you have a girlfriend or something?"

"Nothing is more important to your mom than your well-being." The backpack bounced against her chest and she nearly dropped it.

"Give me the dog, and I'll put it back."

Tears rolled down her cheeks. She tightened her hold on the bag.

"Listen, I know how you feel, it hurts to lose something you love. When I was eight years old, I came home from school to learn my father had given away our dog—my sister was allergic." He didn't think about it often, so he was surprised by the sudden heaviness in his gut. Not because he grieved his border collie. It was his father's demand that still needled him. *Stop crying like a baby. There are a hellava lot worse things in life than losing a dog.*

Paige looked up at him with horror in her eyes. "He just gave it away without telling you?"

"Yep. I'll tell you what. If you put the dog back and let me take you home, then I'll introduce you to a friend of mine who runs an animal shelter. Maybe she could use an extra hand, if you have time to volunteer."

Paige's face brightened. "For real?"

"Yes, for real. What do you say? Deal?"

She looked at the backpack wiggling and whining in her arms. Behind her, a customer cocked his head and looked around. Josh took Paige's arm and steered her back down the aisle.

"Give him to me, and I'll put him in with his brothers and sisters."

With one last sniff, Paige handed over the backpack.

***

An hour later, Josh arrived home. With Paige delivered to her mother and a shop-lifting charge averted, he hoped to set her up at the animal shelter and feel like a super hero.

He twisted the lid off a bottle of room temperature water, he didn't like it cold, and took a long slug. On the counter between the kitchen and living room, his Japanese fighter fish had its nose up against the fishbowl. Josh gave it a few pellets. "Saturday afternoon, and it's just me and you, Hank." And case notes to finish up, and he needed to make a referral for a family to a meal program.

A light knocking sounded on his front door.

"Hi, Lydia," he said, taking a step back to let her in. Lydia was about ten years older than him, a beautiful woman with high cheekbones, fair skin and a slender build. Her short, blonde hair always looked good, like she'd just come from a salon. Half the time, he couldn't tell if she wore makeup or not, but he suspected she did. She was the kind of woman who liked men to notice her. "What brings you here?"

She squeezed his arm and kissed the air beside his cheek, leaving his eyes stinging from her perfume.

"I'm glad you're home." She slipped the shiny yellow purse off her shoulder and pulled an envelope from the side pocket. "Happy birthday!"

"You didn't have to come all the way into the city to say happy birthday."

"I know, but I was downtown for a spa appointment, so the timing was good. I wanted to do something special for you this year."

That was a switch. Lydia sometimes remembered to wish him happy birthday, but she'd never given him a card. "Gee thanks. I feel special."

"You are special. Open your card."

"Do you want to come in?" He took another step back.

"Sure, but I don't have much time. I went to the market for my mother, and she doesn't like her cheese to get warm." She shrugged off her light jacket as they moved from the foyer to the couch in the living room. "Come on now, open your card."

He did and read the message on the front. "Friends like you come once in a life time." God, he hoped so.

Inside the card was a ticket. "Race of Hearts. What's this?"

"It's a dating race my club is hosting in a couple of weeks."

"Oh, yeah? What's a dating race?"

"Based on compatibility, you'll be partnered with a woman, and the two of you will complete romantic tasks in a race against other couples. The winning couple gets $25,000.00." The prize was sang like a song.

"Race where?"

"In Stonewood Hills. It'll be fun, Josh. Or have you forgotten how to have a good time?"

Since he'd taken over managing the Red Pines Wilderness Program, he had no personal time, but it didn't bother him.

He looked at the date on the ticket. "I don't know. I'm pretty busy with work."

"Good Lord, if you can't pull yourself from that job for one afternoon, you're a lost cause. We're signing you up right now." She pulled her iPhone from her purse.

All work and no play suited him just fine. Some people were wired like that. "Lydia, I need to check—"

"Shush, you're checking nothing. I insist you do this race. We're short a couple bachelors and I need your help." Her thumbs flew over her keyboard. "Just give me a second to activate your ticket."

She knew he'd rearrange his schedule to accommodate her. He always did.

"There . . . done," she said, handing him the phone. "Now, while I use your bathroom, you need to complete the personality profile and answer a couple questions."

He sighed and supposed it wouldn't kill him to take a day off, and he'd be helping Lydia. He filled out the profile and was answering the questions when she returned.

"Are you almost done?" she asked.

"Almost. I'm ranking the things I'd most like to do on a date. Here's a good one—go to a sports game. Yep." He circled the number ten for that question.

"Last one. They gotta be kidding. Show her your solo salsa moves? Hell, no." He circled the number one for that question.

Lydia stood over him until he submitted the entry and handed back her phone. With her jacket slung over her arm, she picked up her purse. "I've got to get mother's cheese home." On her way out the door, she looked back over her shoulder. "You're going to have a good time, Josh. Who knows, the woman you meet during Race of Hearts, may be the woman who changes your life."

CHAPTER THREE

Adair flinched after touching the strand of hair she'd just pulled through her flat iron. "Ouch, that's hot." She sat on a stool in front of her bedroom vanity, her attention drawn by a flash of orange her friend, Jessie, dangled behind her.

"That's why you're not supposed to touch it." Jessie laid a necklace down on the vanity in front of Adair. "I have a confession to make."

Adair set the flat iron down and picked up the necklace. She ran her thumb over the tumbled stone hanging in the middle of a long chain. Cool and smooth. Orange topaz? Orange was a color that softened Adair's heart and Jessie knew it.

"I found the necklace amongst my late grandmother's jewelry," said Jessie. "When I saw it, I knew it would go perfectly with your new dress. So it's yours."

"It's beautiful and unexpected. Thank you. Jessie, why are giving me a necklace?" Ever since Jessie arrived at her apartment twenty minutes ago with coffee and croissants, Adair knew something was up. Chocolate almond croissants could easily be a neon sign flashing: 'eat me for a placating distraction.' Whatever was to come, was not going to be good.

"My grandmother had boxes of jewelry. She always liked you, Adair. She'd be tickled to know you think the piece is beautiful." Jessie smoothed a wisp of blonde hair behind her ear and picked up Adair's hair straightener. "I'll do the back of your head, although why you flatten these curls I don't know."

"Because all afternoon, I'll be racing through town doing who-knows-what kind of challenges. If I don't battle the cursed frizz, when I win Race of Hearts, I'll be remembered as the woman whose hair needed a lion tamer. So, spill. Confess. Get it out already."

"The application to increase your line of credit has been declined," Jessie said.

Defeat blew through Adair's lips. "Shit." She slumped down on the stool. Never mind her hair, she needed to flat iron her frazzled nerve endings. If she sold every hat at the show next Saturday, she'd be able to pay her apartment rent, but the rent on the shop?

Jessie shifted from one foot to the other. "I'm sorry. I wish I had some pull at the bank. I could try and borrow some money for you."

"Absolutely not. I'll be okay." Right, keep thinking that. After the sudden death of her business partner, Adair was scrambling to keep afloat. Five years of dreaming, planning, and designing, she'd not fail without a good fight.

"It's obvious what I have to do. I'll just win the $25,000 prize today."

"You'll win. You and that dress are killing it. Paired with your wit, no one stands a chance."

Adair laughed at the absurdity. With skin so ghoulishly pale, legs so gangly awkward, and eyes spread so wide, Adair could almost see behind her.

She better count on wits today.

"Don't laugh. You never see yourself like others do. The prize money is yours."

Adair tried to believe that was true. She wondered if Jessie knew how desperate Adair's situation was, or if she'd fooled her friend with the excuse she hadn't had time to shop for food. She clenched her hands in her lap. If she'd known how quickly her financial state would tail spin, she never would have purchased the stunning snakeskin print dress.

Maybe she'd get points for style. "I wish you'd signed up for the race, too."

Jessie slid the straightener down a strand of curls. "I couldn't. Even though Adam and I may not be on the same page, I can't see myself getting naked with another guy today."

As she had the exact opposite thought. Excitement ran through her nerves at the playfulness, the risqué of partnering with a stranger for the sexy competition. How far would she go to win?

She fixed her posture. "Getting naked is not a requirement of the race, you know."

"No, but it is an R-rated race, and the rules did say the race is not for the shy or prudish."

"Of which you are neither," Adair pointed out.

"True, but I don't want to date another man. Adam is perfect in so many ways, I thought he was the one."

"You thought?" Adair picked up her mascara brush and leaned forward to blacken her strawberry blonde lashes. They looked ridiculous unless darkened to match her raven-in-a-box hair.

"Last night when I told him I was falling for him, he looked at me with a sexy enough smile to melt lead and said: 'Don't do that, baby. No falling.'"

Adair's response hit a blockade on her tongue. *Don't take that frivolous relationship seriously. Don't give Adam your heart. Don't settle for a man who hasn't fallen for you.* She couldn't get the words out. She couldn't hurt her friend with the truth.

"Any man who doesn't fall for you is crazy, Jessie."

"I know." Jessie smiled like sunshine on a rainy day. "I also know Adam and I are perfect for each other, he just needs time to come to that same realization. You know men."

She did, sort of, but she didn't agree. When Adair fell for a man, she wanted him falling right back. She sure as heck wasn't going to wait until he decided not to fall.

Jessie put the hair straightener down and stood back to admire her work. "You are stunning."

Adair stopped herself before she rolled her eyes. She didn't need to be stunning to feel good about herself. Some girls stunned a crowd with beauty and some girls wowed them with other attributes. Like . . . creative talent. Creativity was a winning characteristic. Her mother said so.

"I thought the race started at 1:00. Aren't you going to be late?"

Adair's gaze snapped to the clock on her bedside table. "I have to be there by 12:30. It's only 11:30, I have time."

"I think your clock stopped. My watch says 12:30."

Adair's heart pumped a shot of adrenaline clear to her toes. She jumped up. "What the—? No, it can't be."

She plucked her watch off her vanity. "Dear God in heaven, you're right."

CHAPTER FOUR

Josh handed over his contest entry form to a girl sitting behind the Race of Hearts registration table at the Cushion Club. As he waited, his gaze wandered over the feminine milieu milling around the reception area and landed on one woman in stilettos whose dress stuck to her thighs like wallpaper.

Blood started to thrum through his veins.

Sexy, but stilettos for a race? Not a good partner.

He checked out a woman to their right. Now, this was better. Slim body, clad in jeans and T-shirt, practical shoes, athletic looking, nice b—

"Okay, you're good."

Josh's attention drew back to the registration girl. "Our sponsors, Rosedale Estate Wines, want to thank you for competing in Race of Hearts today. I'm supposed to ask if you could spare a couple minutes to answer a few questions?"

A young woman stepped forward with a clipboard. A yellow, neon clip held black hair off a round face brimming with nervous energy. Dressed in a black and yellow striped shirt, she reminded him of a bumblebee. "Please. I need to gather data for an undergrad assignment." She gave him a look only young adults could pull off, one that screamed the future of our entire species rides on this moment.

He guessed she'd not collected much data. It took nerve at that age to talk to strangers. "Sure, okay. What do you want to know?"

"Can you tell me why you entered the race? Was it for the prize, or was it for love?"

"I'm in this for the prize." Awe damn, that sounded shallow. "Not that there's anything wrong with love. Perhaps love waits for me right now at the first hole." Damn again, that sounded ridiculous on many levels. "I'm here for the adventure, the race, the competition, you know?"

"If you win today, what will you do with the prize money?" Her gaze was sharp. "Something original, I hope, not paying off debts."

Paying off a debt was his only goal. He sighed. Like he could ever expect to end that obligation. "I'll give it to a friend, someone who has a dream I'd like to see come true."

"Pretty decent of you," she said. "I wouldn't mind being your friend. Is this person a woman? Man?"

"A woman, but shhhh, no names. I don't want to raise false hopes." Josh shot her a wink.

Her eyebrows shot up. "So you've already got someone special in your life. What if you get caught with another woman today? They're saying things could get hot between partners."

She wanted a scandal. A wave of indignity rippled through his body. "You think it's smart to jump to that conclusion after talking to me for ten seconds? Why don't you set a higher standard for your paper? Maybe try for accuracy, professionalism, and fairness for starters."

Her eyebrows flattened out. "Thanks for your time. Go outside to the golf course. They'll be announcing the teams in about ten minutes."

He took one step.

"Break a leg, not a heart," the girl added as he moved on.

"Now I'm a heartbreaker," Josh grumbled as he left the clubhouse. Last year, New Perspective magazine called him an innovative social worker who put people before policy, a man whose initiative transformed a community by bringing old world honor and integrity into the lives of troubled teens.

You're not a bad guy.

He headed outside, past the row of golf carts, and wandered over to where a crowd had gathered under a cloudless sky. A black flag with pink hearts fluttered from a pole stuck in the first hole. Carrying the scent of cut grass, the light breeze was one of the first warm ones of the spring.

A couple minutes later, the men were asked to gather on the left side of the green while the women gathered on the right.

He caught the gaze of a dark-haired woman who smiled, a pretty friendly smile, too. She ran her teeth over her lower lip. In the sun, her hair had crimson streaks too perfectly striated to be natural. He liked them. He liked her ASIC's and the way her leggings fit tight to her curves. She looked like a runner, like she had a competitive spirit. Most of the women looked fit enough to run, a level playing field.

One of the contest coordinators whistled to get everyone's attention. "Welcome everyone to the Cushion Club's 5th annual Race of Hearts. We know you're all anxious to meet your partners, so let's get these rules over with. The race is four hours, and in case you've forgotten, you're racing for $25,000.00!"

Lots of excitement over this. Josh added a whistle.

"To celebrate our fifth year, for the winners, we're also throwing in a free romantic weekend at Cushion Club resort as well as a full spa treatment."

Nice. He'd heard the club was private, pristine and posh.

"Okay, on to the rules."

Josh listened until his attention was diverted by a squeal. An orange hat sailed off the head of a dark-haired woman heading toward the group. When she bent over, Josh's gaze fixed on Junoesque legs encased in dark stockings that led up to a dress stretching over a nicely shaped ass. Sleek yet curvaceous. With her hand planting the hat to her head, she ran the last few steps to join the rest of the contestants.

Spunky, fresh, but the dress was no good. Late to the race wearing a hat that didn't stay put. Josh filed her in the same category as the woman in stilettos. The hope-nots.

He stepped closer to the crimson-streaked runner and sent her a smile before turning his attention back to the announcer.

"A reminder—this is an R-rated race, but you dictate the heat level, consensually, whatever you and your partner are comfortable with. Nudity is fine with the judges. May get you a few extra points, may make the difference between a win and a loss. I'm just saying. You have our written guarantee pictures will not be shared and will be deleted after they're judged."

"We want you all to have a great time. Meet someone new, maybe find true love, maybe join the Cushion Club. And now, what you've all been waiting for, it's time to partner you ladies and gents and start the race."

Josh shifted from one foot to the other as five couples were matched before his name was called. The crimson-streaked woman shot him a hopeful smile when he walked past her toward the announcer.

If luck was on his side—

He heard the name of his partner—Adair Ellis—and raised an eyebrow. *Is it you, Crimson Beauty?* The woman sighed and shook her head. Shame.

Through the crowd, he saw a woman heading his way.

The orange hat came forward. He tried not to grimace.

"Another good looking couple." The announcer handed Josh a small backpack. "Don't open this until everyone is paired."

Josh gave his partner a sideways look-over as they moved away.

"Nice to meet you. Are you as pumped as I am?" Adair may have punctuality issues, but she did have a smile about as wide as the sky. He couldn't help reflect one back. At least she didn't have a wimpy handshake.

"You bet. We're going to win this, Adair."

"I know we are. You look familiar to me. I wonder if we've met."

She didn't look familiar to him. "Maybe. I used to live in Stonewood Hills as a kid, but it's been nearly fifteen years since I moved out of the suburbs and into the city."

"I've lived here forever. Perhaps we went to the same school? I didn't catch your name."

Sure, perhaps. He could talk about high school like a normal person. No longer did his stomach clench at the topic and his mind scream avoid. "I went to Crestfield High."

"I did, too."

"I'm Josh Cohen."

Her eyes had squinted out the sun. Now they flared open, and then wider still, wide enough to make him take a step back.

CHAPTER FIVE

Shit. Shit. Shit!

It was him. That Josh. He so didn't look like his teenaged self. But he still looked good. Really good.

Act normal! Smile. Swallow. Tell a lie. "I'm wrong. I was thinking of someone else. I know I'm mistaken because in high school I did nothing socially, so we couldn't have met . . . never." Right, that was subtle.

Ker-thump. Ker-thump. Unless a town parade of steel drum bands crossed the golf course right now, he would hear her heart banging against her ribcage.

He studied her with questioning eyes. Go figure. She'd made herself sound like a loser, a social misfit, a reject. *Lies never make things better.* "What I meant was I spent all my time in . . . in competitive kayaking, every morning, every afternoon, every day. I had to be in bed at nine o'clock to get up for the six am practices. That left time for nothing other than schoolwork. You know how it is when you're training." *Stop rambling. Take a breath.*

"Actually no, I don't." Now he looked amused.

"Well, it's intense." Her heart pumped blood furiously through her lungs. *No, don't hyperventilate.* Of all the people on the planet. What were the odds she'd be partnered with Josh Cohen? Why did their stars have to align now?

"You look pretty worked up just at the memory, I can only imagine." His gaze dropped to her feet.

"Can you run in those shoes?"

Adair looked down. She had no idea what shoes she'd slipped on. Good news, they matched. Bad news, three-inch wedges. "Yes, I run in these all the time." Another deception. She should keep an eye peeled for tangled webs.

Dressed in steel-grey board shorts and a striped shirt under a navy colored jacket, Josh was shod in sensible, silver Nikes. He still had the physique of an athlete, wide shoulders, lean hips, muscled, toned, skin like amber.

"Okay, contestants, can I have your attention?" came the booming voice of the contest coordinator. Thank the powers that be.

Adair tried not to breathe like a drowning victim and eyed a woman's cobalt blue runners.

Wait, why was she freaking out? He didn't know who she was. He'd never known who she was.

Her heartbeat lightened up to a rat-a-tat-tat.

Besides, she didn't look anything like seventeen-year-old Adair. Curls that had been strawberry blonde, were now flattened straight and dyed indigo black.

She released an exhale from way down deep, but it wasn't quite enough to settle her nerves.

The announcer was talking. Did she miss anything?

"Damn," Josh said. "No way I'm doing that, so we better move our butts."

Doing what? Good grief, what had she missed?

"When I blow this whistle, open your backpacks, read your first task, and get moving. You have until 1:30 to complete that task."

"We have forty minutes," Josh said.

Adair caught his eye, one glance that said we're in this together, and she felt a solar burst in her chest.

The boy who'd had a huge impact on her life, the boy she'd lost countless hours of sleep over, the boy she never expected to see again, was now a man. All man. All sinfully, gorgeous man.

She was seventeen again, panting puppy dog love.

Shifting her position back a bit, she looked him over. Dark hair that used to ripple over his head was now cropped shorter, but it still looked soft—in her fantasies it had always been soft as a bunny.

The piercing shrill of a whistle forced Josh into action. He unzipped the backpack and withdrew an envelope.

"Your first task," he read, "is to drive to the Assiniboine Yacht Club where you'll find a variety of conveyances to take you up the river to Eagle Point Park. At the park you must find a citizen to take a video of your first kiss. Send the video to your contact and you'll receive your next task."

"A kiss." Said without swooning as she became more firmly planted in reality."Looks like we're not wasting time. How do we know who our contact is?"

Josh started to jog. "Details in the backpack. If you'd been on time, you'd know that. Let's go. My car."

He'd said it with a smile, but that comment knocked a cloud in front of the sunshine. "I know I was late. I'm sorry." She started to run behind him, in heels. Why couldn't she have stuffed her runners on as she flew out the door? She willed her feet to be steady as they raced from the green through the parking lot to a modest, black Mazda. Adair jumped in the passenger side.

Josh tossed her the backpack. "We'll be at the river in 5 minutes. While I drive, you can look through the bag."

She may have been late to the race, but she didn't need to be told what to do.

He'd been backing up the car, but he paused for a second and gave her a look that took away all the hard edges on his face. "Sorry, I'm not the boss here."

The last thing she wanted was tension between them. As they left the parking lot, she looked back to see cars bottlenecked along the one driveway out of the Cushion Club. "Good planning to park close to the exit."

"I like to think ahead. Anything important in there?"

She leafed through the backpack. "We didn't get much. Water, a couple of energy bars, notebook and a pen. Oh, this is interesting: a sealed envelope that says do not open, and—good grief!—condoms. A twelve-pack, no less."

Josh looked at her and grinned.

Sex had been a mystery back in high school, nothing more than a few sloppy kisses from overzealous boys who tried to grope her breasts. Now, she knew what to do with a condom.

"Presumptuous," he said.

Her hormones torpedoed out of hibernation and set a trajectory for Josh and mind-blowing sex.

Dream come true?

Or nightmare?

Better pull back the reign on her hormones . . . just a bit. If she intended to keep history buried, their relationship could go no deeper than mind-blowing sex. "I think we should use every resource to win this race."

He shot her a smile that was both sizzling and sweet. "I like your thinking."

Her shoulders relaxed a little more. They'd gotten off to a rocky start, but there was no reason they couldn't sail smooth from here.

They reached the river within five minutes. The tributary emptied into the great lake, but they'd be headed up river to Stonewood Hill's claim to fame, the Eagle Point Amusement Park that drew visitors from afar.

Josh parked the car on the street. "I see the flag by the water. By the way, you look incredible in that dress." He grabbed the backpack out of her lap. "Come on, Adair, time to get those high-heels moving."

"Don't worry, these heels will keep up to yours just fine." She hoped that was true. The sight of another couple leaping out of a car was fire under her feet.

On one side of the road were two-story apartments above shops, a cafe, and a restaurant. They headed the other way toward the yacht club, running across the cobblestone boardwalk past boxed gardens to the public docks.

Adair's heart plummeted as she looked over the assortment of conveyances lined up at the water's edge— a couple small sailboats, canoes, row-boats, pedal boats and kayaks.

She gaped at the kayaks. Seriously. Kayaks? What kind of bad luck was this?

"What kind of great luck is this?" Josh lifted the kayak over his head in one graceful move and tilted his head to peek at her. "Grab the paddles please, partner. How many races did you win?"

"It's difficult to keep track of those things." Sweat trickled down between her shoulder blades as she slipped the backpack on. "You know, it's been a long time since I've been in one of these." Good Lord, which end was up? "And I should mention I suffered a shoulder injury, cut my career short, and I haven't paddled since the . . . psychologically, traumatizing loss." She swallowed hard and rubbed her left shoulder. "I can still feel it some days."

She'd been in a kayak once in her life, briefly, as long as it took to tip and dunk headfirst into the water. Please no, she prayed. Not today. Bedraggled was a terrible look for her.

He slipped the boat into the water off the dock and crouched by the back end to hold it in place. "You want the front or back position?"

"Oh, it doesn't matter, front, back, middle." Upside down, all equally bad. "I paddled them all." Liar, liar, liar. What was wrong with her?

"Okay, I'll take the back."

She scanned the water, praying for a kayaker to speed by, so she could figure out how to grip the paddle. She glanced at the other couple. The guy was helping the woman into the kayak. But competitive kayaker Adair shouldn't need assistance.

Bracing herself with a hand on the side, she stepped in. Oh dear, the thing was wobbly. It jerked to the side. She stifled a squeal in her throat as the paddle swung up and knocked her in the chin. Easy does it.

"Are you okay there?"

Her glance back at Josh was just long enough to catch the perplexed look on his face. *You're puzzled now, Josh? You ain't seen nothing yet.* She should have taken the back position, so he couldn't watch her. "I'm fine. I never wore sandals like this when I kayaked."

Other couples had arrived. They would lose their lead if she didn't hurry.

Adair held her breath. With her hands gripping both sides of the boat, she steadied it, stepped in and crouched down to sit. The kayak lurched to one side as a screech tore her throat. The kayak kept tipping. Her forearm hit the water. Cold seeped through the sleeve of her jean jacket.

Her next breath was a choke. Time rolled out slowly as her mind conjured up a ruined dress. Ruined makeup. Ruined hair, as if Fate had reached out, found Adair Ellis and with a big belly laugh, tipped the scales, the boat, and the circumstances.

Total ruination!

Just like she'd ruined Josh's life.

CHAPTER SIX

Josh had his hand on the grab handle at the stern of the kayak as Adair stepped in. The vessel lurched to the left, taking him by surprise, but he held tight. Adair didn't tip. Experienced kayaker?

"Good grief! Thank you, Josh." Adair could be sitting on thistles if he was reading her comfort level right. She squeezed water from the sleeve of her jacket. "That could have been disastrous."

"It's been awhile for you, I guess. You must be rusty." He used his paddle like a brace across the sides of the boat to steady himself as he stepped into the middle of the kayak.

She looked over her shoulder at him. "I hope it's like riding a bike."

"Grab your paddle. Let's go." He pushed away from the dock and dug into the water. "We'll go straight up the middle until we see the park."

He watched her paddle so he could match the rhythm of her stroke. Would have been nice if she had any rhythm. The left side of her paddle barely skimmed the water while the right side dug in too deep. He corrected by paddling the left side.

Behind them, other contestants yelled to each other as they chose their boats.

Luckily they didn't have far to go. The park was a ten-minute paddle at most. He spared a glance back and saw the couple who'd grabbed the kayak gaining on them. He and Adair were going to lose their lead.

"Come on, Adair. Faster. Give it all you've got."

She dug her paddle into the water in a sloosh-thwap, sloosh-thwap cacophonic measure. His dismay turned to horror when the paddle slipped from her grasp. Gaping, he watched as she tried to snatch it back, but missed.

"Shiza!" she cried. The paddle hit the water as the front of the kayak sailed past.

He dug in on the left side, muscles straining as he reached to grab the tip and ignore the ribbing from the canoe that passed.

She'd raced as many kayaks as he'd raced fighter jets. He tossed the paddle up to Adair.

Harder. Faster. Eyes on the shore. Right side. Left side. Right side. Left side.

They were neck-in-neck with a rowboat. Irritation wiped the smile from his face along with any expectation of further dates with Adair. Trust a woman who lied? Not a chance.

Two yahoos in a speedboat sped past as he steered them toward a landing pad on the left side of the docks. He was out of his shoes in three seconds. The water was only knee deep, so he vaulted out of the kayak. Master that she was, she didn't need his help. "I'll run ahead and find someone to take the picture we need."

"Sure. Go. I'll catch up."

With his shoes stuffed on, he started to run. Ten paces later, he heard Adair's screech.

A curse left his lips when he stopped and looked back. Waves rolling toward the shore from the speedboat hit the kayak as Adair exited. One wave too many and she toppled over the side. As she disappeared from view, his heart pumped a shot of adrenaline through his veins.

Damn! What an ass he was.

He shot back to the kayak. He saw those waves coming, knew she was a novice. Hadn't mattered. He'd left her anyway.

By the time he hit the water, Adair, sputtering and stumbling, had gotten to her feet, a look of horror on her pale, dripping face.

He steadied her with a grip on her forearm and helped her the few steps to shore. "Are you okay, did you hurt yourself?"

Either shock or humiliation or both had flash-frozen any words trying to escape her gaping mouth. She'd not gone all the way under as he'd first thought, although much of her dribbled. Some of her hair was spared by the floppy hat she'd worn. A hat she rescued and shook out as she surveyed her jacket and pretty dress.

"I . . . I . . I can't believe that happened. No, I didn't hurt myself. I'll be fine, really, it's just a little fish water." She ran her fingers through her drippy hair. "No hairbrush, no makeup. Oh man, I bet you can't wait to kiss me now."

He couldn't help smiling as she looked down at her glistening shoes. Relief washed through him to know she wasn't hurt, yet he wasn't exactly in a kissing mood. Chances were good, she'd lied about racing kayaks. Who'd lie about something like that?

"No time to worry about your hair." He picked up the backpack and took her hand to get her moving. "You're shivering." With a glance toward the river, just a sailboat still to dock as far as he could tell, he whipped off his jacket. They'd lost their lead by a long shot. "Here, wear mine. And let's run. You'll warm up."

She didn't miss a step, changing jackets as she jogged. "I don't often wear makeup, but I was so picky this morning, getting the perfect shade of eye shadow, as if it matters."

He wouldn't dismiss she'd lied, but he did like that she cared about details. And he liked how she recovered quickly. No dramatics. "Some men don't mind their women wet, Adair."

She dropped her eyelids in a flirtatious gesture that warmed him up. "I guess you've figured out why I quit kayaking. Not my forte. I was never a great asset to my team."

"Even the pros take a tumble once in a while."

While they closed the distance to the ferry, his mind strayed to the prize, to how good it would feel to hand over the winnings. He wondered if it'd be good enough to save his soul.

If he and Adair intended to impress the judges, their kiss better be good, even if he wasn't feeling it.

"Where's a willing citizen when you need one?" Adair continued running past the dock until she reached the path that led into the park.

He took off after her. Impressive. She was in great shape, not winded at all. Maybe she was still thinking about the kiss. He imagined the feel of his lips meeting hers, how the curves of her body would fit against him.

Her words popped into his head. *I spent all my time in competitive kayaking, every morning, every afternoon, every day.* The fantasy kiss vanished from his imagination. Just make it look good for the prize.

As they turned a corner, he saw a couple groups of people. "Finally. Let's ask that guy in the red shirt."

"No, not him, Josh. He has little kids, it's not appropriate."

"Right, good call."

"Let's get that couple in front of them." Adair's shoes squeaked with each step.

"Okay, squeegee, get ready to pucker up," Josh said.

Adair shot him a look then stopped him with a tug to his arm. "Wait, let's think about this for a second. This shouldn't just be a kiss, we want to stand apart from the other contestants. How can we play to the romance aspect of this race?"

"I have an idea. You grab that couple before they get away."

Trees were in spring bloom, edging the trail with some kind of flowers, white with pink centres. Good enough. He sidetracked to a tree and picked one of the blossoms.

When he caught up to Adair, she was explaining the race to the couple and asking them to take the picture. Josh pulled his phone from his pocket and handed it to the guy.

Adair scanned the park. "Let's put the river behind us, it's pretty with that church spire on the hill." She was right. He wouldn't have thought about a background.

Their impromptu photographer agreed. "The shot looks great from here. Okay, video's rolling, let's see what you've got."

Adair reached for him, but instead of meeting her with his lips, he took her hand and kissed it first. Her hand was cold, so he let his lips linger, breathing warmth over her chilled skin.

Her hair had begun to dry into ringlets with a brilliant obsidian sheen in the sunlight. He brushed a curl from her temple, took the blossoms he'd picked and poked the stem in behind her ear, so the flowers framed the side of her face. "You look pretty. Blossoms fade in comparison to you, Adair."

Her face lit when she smiled. "I doubt that, but thanks for seeing past my drizzle and for being the king of corny."

The look of desire in her eyes was inviting. Adair wanted him to kiss her, he felt it in the way her breathing picked up, and despite his reservations, he might find a way to enjoy this kiss.

CHAPTER SEVEN

Even though a drip plunked onto Adair's cheek, she tried not to melt into a puddle when Josh Cohen's lips approached hers. Her mind was a medley of sweet reminiscences, taking her back on a stream of young yearning to her seventeenth year. All the feelings of her life-altering crush on Josh woke with the fervor of a fairy-tale princess rising from a cursed sleep.

A kiss.

She'd wanted Josh's kiss so badly it hurt her soul.

The park began to blur as she focussed on his eyes. As a teenager, she'd always believed that kissing Josh would cause tectonic plates to collide. Or at the very least, angels to break into heavenly chorus and the sun to shoot to its zenith no matter the time of day.

As a grown woman, she'd come to believe that earth-shattering kisses were the stuff and nonsense of fairy tales.

Wrong. She knew it when his lips met hers. She slipped into his kiss like she was changing worlds. Her tummy clenched in an exquisite response from the second his hand cupped the back of her head in a dominating hold. Erotic as hell coming from Josh.

His tongue played across her lips then delved inside to meet hers. He tasted of sinfully dark nights and fire lit passion.

His kiss was demanding, take-charge, possessive, all things unexpected. As unexpected as the soft whimper escaping her throat. Her senses expanded to take in the feel of his shoulders, lean and broad. God, she loved the feel of hard muscle, as if it spoke to her primal this-man-can-protect-you femininity.

His clean masculine scent was infused with sandalwood, a scent that surrounded her. She wanted to breathe him in. The deft way he used the tip of his tongue was a flame through her body as much as his kiss was a hot caress of her mouth.

Yes, hot.

Until her brain doused cold water over her fantasy. It was not okay to turn this kiss into a dramatic moment. Losing herself to Josh once was enough.

Yet she couldn't part. As if he'd bonded her to him from nothing more than the touch of his lips, the kiss consumed her whole body.

Her fingers slipped up the back of his neck and through his hair. Yes, as she'd thought, sensually soft against the inside of her fingers. Just one more minute and she would have her fill.

When he pulled back, the heady sensation lingered. If she had no understanding of chemical reactions before, she did now. He set off effects that ping-ponged through her body. Attraction. Terror. Lust. Remorse. Her mind scrambled for words.

They'd been together less than an hour and she'd already lied to him. This relationship was doomed before it began.

Don't go there. Don't regurgitate that guilt.

"That was a pretty awesome kiss, Adair."

She nodded, fearing her voice would crack. *Focus on his eyes.* Or maybe not. Was there a man on the planet more able to buckle her knees with his eyes?

Looking away, she suddenly realized how lucky she was. This day with Josh was a gift. Not just because he'd turned her into a flaming crème brûlée, but because now she knew Josh was okay. Any man who kissed like that was not on the verge of self-destruction. And if he was okay, then maybe she could stop hating herself for ruining his life.

"If that wasn't a winning kiss," Josh said, "I don't know what qualifies."

A winning kiss? As in staged. Rote. Forced? The earth didn't shift even a little for him? Of course not. Why should it? It's all part of the game. *Get your head out of the Milky Way, Adair.*

"I think I got it all," said the guy who'd been taking the video. "Want to take a look?" He gave the camera back to Josh and wished them good luck.

They ran the video back as Adair leaned into Josh for a better view. A low, sexy rumble sounded in his throat when the camera zoomed in. "Looks pretty good. He got in nice and close."

They did look pretty good and pretty lost. Adrift in that kiss. Watching it was like reliving it. He moved closer and his hip brushed against hers.

"Yes, we did make it look real," she said.

It would have been nice if he'd said the kiss was real. Instead, a frown flickered at the edges of his mouth and then it was gone.

He shifted away from her and scrolled through his email. "At least we're early, just by four minutes though. Where do we send the picture?"

It was just a mediocre kiss. She tore through the backpack looking for their instructions. *That kiss a few years back in the elevator with Willy Agnew, now that was steam heat.*

"Hurry, Adair. I'm not performing that elimination challenge, so we better not be in last place."

Elimination challenge? She must have missed those details when she'd been having her panic attack. "I agree, me neither," she said, trying to look convincing and not bewildered as she retrieved the instructions. "A little damp, but readable." She gave him the number of their contact at the Cushion Club and scanned the rest of the note on the chance it mentioned an elimination challenge—nothing.

Please, let us not be last. Especially not after that kayaking fiasco. That thought brought another problem to mind.

As he sent the picture, she pulled her fingers through her now drying curls. Curls reminiscent of seventeen-year-old Adair. And what about her freckles, the ones that felt like weights across her nose? Did she have makeup left on those self-incriminating spots? He hadn't remembered her name, but what if her appearance sparked a memory despite her bottled black hair?

A tune rang from his phone. "That's Hakuna Matata. From the Lion King." Joyful and unexpected. The tension in her shoulders let go a little.

"Yeah, no worries and all that." Josh read the text message that arrived. "You came in sixteenth place."

"How many teams are there?"

"Eighteen. I got another text. For your next task, you must text back one of your names." He looked at her and smiled. "That's a relief. We're still in this. I'll send my name."

Relieved and renewed, Adair combed her fingers through her hair some more.

Moments later another message came back. He read it aloud, "Joshua, you will compose an ode to Adair. Write a poem that expresses your admiration for one of Adair's physical attributes. You write while she takes you back across the lake. Email your poem for your next task. You have fifteen minutes."

"Poetry? I should have paid attention in English Lit."

They ran back to the shore. Her enthusiasm diminished when she saw quite a few couples already skimming down the river.

She cringed as they reached the kayaks. Her feet still squeaked in her shoes. She peeled them off, tossed them into her little cockpit, and snatched up the paddle. "I'll sit in the back this time, so you can concentrate on your poem."

Josh looked tense as he spun the kayak around. "I haven't written anything resembling poetry since fifth grade. The only poems I know start with roses are red. Paddle your heart out, Adair. Let's get back our lead."

She would not think about how desperately she needed to win. Desperate people made mistakes. They were back on the river in seconds. Although it was chilly, she warmed up quickly as she set her sights ahead and dug the paddle in hard. She had a better feel for it now, her strokes pulled through the water more fluid and even.

Chances were pretty good that he'd caught on to the, I'm-a-champion-kayaker lie. Why did the two lies she'd told in her life revolve around Josh Cohen? Because she'd woven a tangled web of deception. That's how the saying went.

The lies stopped now. This was a second chance, a chance to untangle. She would make up for her deceptions by being the best partner he could have. Whatever it took, she was master of her fate—no one was more committed to winning.

"You're not shy are you?" he called back to her. "You want to give the judges something racy?"

People who risked nothing, never knew how far they could have gone. "I'm not shy. Go for it."

Josh let go a few belly laughs as they headed downstream. She wondered what he had in mind, and if truth be told, she'd had a few exhibitionist fantasies just like many other woman, she just lacked opportunity. Paying the bills meant working every waking hour and some of the sleeping ones, too.

She nearly lost her hat when he started to paddle with speed enough to reach land with no more than half the other teams. He must have finished his poem.

Josh jumped out of the kayak with athletic grace she could only hope to mimic, but didn't require since he pulled the kayak aground and lent his hand. Luckily her dress was lightweight and had pretty much dried. At least the sun shone warm in the sky. He already had his phone out, and his fingers flew over the buttons typing out his ode as she put on her shoes.

"Oh man, this is bad," he said with a grimace. "The sad part is, I couldn't have done any better if I'd had a month to write this thing."

She tried to peek over his shoulder, but he waggled his eyebrows at her and turned his back. Some of the other couples were heading to their cars, so Josh and Adair did the same.

"I can't wait any longer. Come on, let's hear it."

"Okay, here goes: There was a hot babe from Stonewood Hills. Whose bosom inspired men's quills. Fair of skin, ample breast, her pleasure was my quest. And to keep her bod warm against wind chills."

Adair couldn't help her laugh. "Wind chills?"

"It was all I could think of considering the topple you took. It could have been worse, I had ripple and nipple to work with."

Her pleasure was my quest. Truly? Or was it just a line in a poem. "A breast man, huh?"

"Indeed."

Her knees gave a little tremble at the notion Josh might desire her. She could pretend for one day, couldn't she? *Oh, how this man pursues me relentlessly.* The fantasy cheered her up.

She had a good idea what the next challenge would be, but could she do it? The tightening deep in her belly, the one that made her want to squeeze her thighs together answered with a vampish yes.

CHAPTER EIGHT

Excitement and apprehension hummed through Josh as he read the next message from their Cushion Club contact.

"What do we have to do?" asked Adair.

He shook his head. "It's too risky."

"What is?"

"For bonus points, they're suggesting we send in a picture to accompany ode to Adair within ten minutes."

Adair's cheeks were back in the pink. The way she flitted her eyelashes at him was seductive as hell. "So let me get this straight. Your vote is for us forfeiting bonus points?"

"Opposed to you stripping down on the streets of Stonewood Hills?" That image provoked every carnal fantasy he'd ever had. "As much as I'd love to take that picture, there's no privacy here, and it's not worth an indecent exposure charge."

"Oh, come on. We won't get caught." Adair scanned the parking lot. "Is there something wrong with me that I find a little public exposure kind of exciting?"

"More than kind of and no, but that dress looks complicated. You can't just give a quick flash—"

"Good grief," she said, checking her watch. "How can we be artistic with only ten minutes?"

Like boobs weren't an art form on their own. "Artistic is the least issue here."

Her gazed dropped to the rusted bin beside them. "This garbage has to go. Let's try over there by that tree." Adair took off before he could protest.

When she reached the old maple, she stood with her back to the tree trunk, lips turned in a frown. "It's shadier than I thought. Not enough light."

He looked across the lawn to the pathway. About fifty feet away, a couple people walked toward them. "Take a few steps to the right. No one will see you under that branch."

She gave him a look. "What's the point of taking a picture no one can see?" She bit her lip and ducked out from under the tree. "We need a good backdrop. We have to win this."

"I want to win too, but—"

"I have an idea. See the sunbeam hitting the ground on the other side of that wall. Maybe we can get a decent effect with the light if I stand there."

"The wall? Are you kidding me? It's out in the middle of everything."

But she didn't listen. Bloody woman, she took off again. He scooted after her to the wall.

On the sunshine side, someone had painted a mural in bold colors of the faces found in their multi-cultural province.

"This is perfect!" she cried. "Quick, unzip me." She turned her back to him, but not before he'd seen the thrill in her eyes. Damn, that look of excitement was viral.

His attention snapped to her zipper and suddenly his mind filled with breasts. God, she was bold, adventurous, confident, and she was right. The backdrop was incredible and would make an exceptional shot.

He looked up and down the boardwalk.

His fingers fumbled on her zipper, like a jittery teenager unzipping his first dress. Lowering her zipper was a fuse through his blood, sending it on a downhill plummet to his groin.

Another quick glance along the boardwalk.

He lifted her hair off her neck. Skin like moonstone, so smooth, he had to touch. Whatever cream she'd applied made her shimmer in the sun. Accompanied by a light flowery scent, she had crazy appeal. He kissed a sun-warmed freckle on her shoulder as the zipper reached the bottom. Irresistible. When he slipped the dress off her shoulders, he sensed how still she'd become.

The way she tilted her head and exposed a greater length of her neck tantalized him even more. He didn't fumble when he slipped her bra straps off and opened the clasp, but man, he'd never experienced a buzz like this.

"Your lips made me tremble all the way to my toes."

Another glance down the street ratcheted up his heartbeat when he realized nothing had registered from his last glances. A guy was coming their way, and Josh had no idea how long he'd been there. "We better hurry up."

She turned to face him. Her front teeth pulled across her bottom lip as she pushed her dress down so it puddled just under her breasts. "I can't believe I'm doing this." She leaned back into the wall, one arm up behind her head. "I can't believe how freaking exciting this is either. Don't get the whole dress in the shot."

Dress? What dress? He couldn't think. She was exquisite, but it was her smile that enticed. Playful, seductive, teasing. Incredibly hot. It took all his self-control not to step forward and take one of her hardening coral-colored nipples into his mouth, tease her back. Her full breasts were beautifully shaped, not too big for her small frame. With her skin shimmering in the sun, the picture would be spectacular.

"Were you planning on taking a picture today?"

"Yeah, any second now, but just so you know, I'll still have this vision in my head on my deathbed."

Her moonstone skin stood out against the colors in the bold mural, and that hat of hers was the sexiest thing. He couldn't imagine a more organic backdrop. The shot was beautiful. He took a couple quick ones from different angles.

And then—footsteps. What was he thinking, getting distracted like this? The guy approaching had his gaze trained on the naked beauty against the wall.

"Did you get it?" Adair asked, still stuck in her stance. "Is this a good pose?"

"Spectacular pose." The guy chimed in, wide smile for Adair.

"Move along, buddy." An unexpected possessiveness flared up before Adair covered up.

"Hey, this isn't a bedroom. You don't want me to look, tell your girlfriend to keep her clothes on."

"Or you could go fu—"

His retort was cut off when Adair yanked his sleeve, her dress back in place. "Perhaps pencil in a date on your calendar for an arm wrestle, we don't have time today."

He took a deep breath. "Right, sorry, I'm not usually a Neanderthal. You know you made his day." Josh's jealousy was a surprise. He had no reason to feel possessive, especially not over a woman who didn't respect the truth.

She slipped her arm through his. When she shifted, her breast pressed against his arm as he quickly showed her the pictures. He'd never been more aware of a breast, more aware of wanting to touch breasts. Her breasts filled his head. It wasn't the size or shape that was so damn provocative, it was her attitude, the fact she'd invited him to look. That provocation was sexy as all hell. Damn, the woman had him running hot and cold.

"I think the last one is best," she said.

"Huh?"

"You don't think so?"

"Yeah." He turned his attention to the camera. "Sweet mercy, woman."

She was right. In the picture, she'd turned her shoulder, and a ray of sunlight touched the tip of her nipple. Outstanding.

His entire body tightened in a lust clench around his balls.

Once the picture was sent, he tipped her head back and closed his lips over hers. She tasted better than every rare treat he'd ever devoured. He was conscious of her hands, how they moved over his shoulders, deliberately, like she was learning every inch of him. Her fingers roamed up the back of his neck, through his hair. But her hands didn't drive him nearly as crazy as the tip of her tongue flickering against his. His senses heightened tenfold once again, and all he wanted to do was spend the rest of the day exploring her body. Everything about her felt fresh like he'd just hibernated through ten winters and it was finally spring.

Hakuna Matata rang from his phone. A message. The race. Damn.

When she pulled her lips away, his felt empty.

He'd been wonder-struck by a kiss.

Because the air sizzled with the promise of sex? Like that hadn't happened before. He pulled the phone from his pocket and read the message. "Well done, Joshua and Adair. You'll have to keep enticing the judges and move faster to win. As you wait for your next task, find out everything you can about your partner."

"I hope we got those bonus points," said Adair. "How many points can we get?"

"We were told each of the seven tasks is awarded up to five points based on punctuality and creativity."

"See, creativity counts."

"True, but I didn't want you getting into trouble."

Adair looked over one shoulder then the other. "I don't see trouble closing in, we're okay. So, we should probably ask deeper questions than what's your favourite color."

"We know yours is orange. I don't have a favourite, maybe grey."

"You've got to be kidding. That's depressing."

"Light grey? What's your dream destination?"

"Scotland," Adair said. "I have a thing for men in kilts. Yours?"

"Egypt. I've always been fascinated by the culture." He wanted to dig deeper. Whether it was a primal instinct surfacing, for reasons he couldn't explain, he wanted to know what made this vivacious woman feel vulnerable. "What makes you cry?"

CHAPTER NINE

Adair didn't have to think twice. Her tears were still fresh. "My cousin died two months ago. We'd always been close and were starting a business together in hats and accessories." She paused, not wanting to talk about her financial situation. "It's still hard to believe she's gone."

"That was a bad question. I didn't mean to open wounds. I'm sorry you lost someone special, Adair."

"Yeah, me too." Her uncle, Elaine's father, hadn't supported this business venture. He thought it reckless of Elaine to leave the security of her job as an insurance broker. Adair didn't want to tarnish Elaine's memory by letting her father know she'd defied his wishes and left Adair in a financial crisis. It was a crisis she'd fix herself.

They started walking back toward the car. "Okay, my turn. What accomplishment are you proud of?" No questions to bring the past roaring back. Nothing to instigate painful memories. She'd rather hear what was good in his life.

"Ah, better question than mine. I'm most proud of my work with troubled teens. I helped establish a wilderness program to teach kids survival skills that translate into daily life competence."

"That's awesome. You must learn a lot from those kids."

"Yeah, it's great to see the kids change both physically and emotionally. They begin to gain self-awareness and believe in themselves. Seeing lives turn around like that, man, it's gratifying."

"That's impressive, Josh. Not many people choose to do that sort of thing."

They reached the shade tree. He stopped walking and ran his hand through his hair. A line creased between his eyes. "I'm not a saint, Adair. I don't usually share this on a first date, but I didn't make the choice that led me to that work. It was court ordered I perform a community service, part of the juvenile restorative justice program. Working with the kids was life-changing in many ways, like a call for me to become a better person, so I continued with it."

Adair closed her mouth. Juvenile justice program. When? Back in high school, everyone talked about Josh's dramatic suicide attempt after Carly broke up with him. Why community service?

"It was a stupid thing I did, and I paid a pretty high price, but I'm happy to say, I've never been stupid again."

Questions tumbled through Adair's mind, but were instantly hushed by her internal mind-your-own-business monitor. She'd reached her lifetime quota of sticking her nose where it didn't belong.

He dropped his gaze to his phone.

"Josh, we've all done things we wished we hadn't, especially as teenagers."

"I don't plan to repeat that mistake. Do you want to have kids?"

Her mind changed direction. With him? A heavenly black-haired cherub popped into her mind. *He didn't mean with you!*

"This must be what speed dating is like. Yes, I want kids, but I'm in no rush. I want to get my business on its feet first. My parents were great advocators of choosing a career you love."

"Sounds like you have pretty decent parents."

She did. Unlike Elaine's parents, Adair's had been proud when she and Elaine had been accepted into the National Artisan's Marketplace trade show this year, another huge expense that reminded her how much she needed to win this race. "What is taking so long? We need to get moving if we're going to win this—"

Hakuna Matata rang out. Another message.

"Yes! Let's get going."

"For your next challenge," Josh read. "It's time to open the sealed envelope in your bag. You have forty minutes to complete this task and text your photo proof."

She leafed through the backpack for the envelope, tore it open and read the note inside. "In this challenge, you must purchase the necessary props for the game outlined on page two of this package. Once you have what you need, persuade a couple you've never met to play the game and send a text to your judge within two hours, giving you a rating between 1 and 10 on their game experience. You may spend no more than $10."

"Ten dollars isn't much," Josh said. "How does the game work?"

She sped-read through the game outline. "It's a role play game. Gives different scenarios and ideas to get started."

"Me Tarzan, you Jane?"

"You'd look good in a loin cloth," she said, running alongside him to the car. "We have to find props for Sleeping Beauty, a bake off, pirates, handy man, and a few others."

When they'd buckled up, Josh turned to her. "Have you ever, you know, played games like that?"

The thrill of stepping into unchartered territory ran under her skin. Fun, discovery, play time with Josh. "No, you?"

"Never. Sounds like fun though, especially with someone with your creative talents." The wink he sent her warmed up all the right parts.

"We'd better start thinking creatively. I think our best bet is a dollar store."

"Lead the way. An image of you in leather just popped into my head."

"I'm seeing you as a fireman." Adair gave directions. "While you drive I'm going to grill you. What's your favourite food?"

"I'll take a side of ribs done pretty much any way. Love 'em. You?"

"My favourite is sushi. What about drinks?"

"Coke not Pepsi," Josh said. "Coffee not tea. Hot chocolate on cold winter nights."

"Can't stand pop. I'm addicted to coffee."

"What kind of books do you like to read?" he asked.

She liked that question. It suggested he read and she loved to discuss novels. "I read a variety, but my favourite would be suspense. If it's romance, all the better. I like a book that leaves me feeling good. You?"

"I like a good drama and have been hooked on WWI novels lately." He stopped the car at a yellow light. She bit back the urge to say go through it! Hard to criticize someone for being a safe driver.

Main St. was lined with shops and restaurants. They drove past shoe stores and a lighting shop with a tavern in between. "We're nearly there. Maybe go just a little faster."

But no. Another yellow light.

The tragedy in their teenage years still hovered in the back of her mind. She may never have another opportunity to learn how her actions had affected him. "Since the theme of this race is romance, I have a question for you. If you could go back to your teenage self and tell him anything about love, what would you tell him?"

"Interesting question. I would tell my teenage self that love is not supposed to have an agenda."

She pushed a little. "You mean having a girlfriend who uses you because you look good on her arm or boost her status?"

"Yeah, I guess so. I wasn't thinking that specifically, but that sort of thing. Being with someone for what they can do for you is not love."

That was surprising. She'd expected something along the lines of don't take lost love too seriously. It might hurt, but you'll get over it. When had Josh realized Carly was using him?

"Turn right at the next light," she said, putting the question aside.

They could have made it through the yellow light, but Josh stopped and waited for a couple cars to go through before he turned.

One, hippopotamus, two hippopotamus, three. Time moved. They didn't. "Hurry, Josh, we don't want to lose points by being late. We have to win this."

"Not worth risking a life, Adair. We're almost there."

Almost is relative. *Step it up a little!* She had the door handle open before they came to a stop. "We better make this good."

Josh grabbed her hand as they met on the sidewalk. "Look. A Naughty and Nice store. Maybe we could get some ideas in there. Find something discounted?"

She checked her watch. They'd not used as much time as she thought. Only five minutes. In the same plaza was a restaurant where they could find a couple to play their game, so they wouldn't have to drive elsewhere.

"Sure, let's look."

Pinks and reds and black décor made the shop look like a burlesque club. She couldn't believe she'd never been in a store like this. She'd become that boring. "This looks like fun."

Josh headed to the centre of the shop where a sign hung over a display—games people play.

Adair couldn't help running her fingers through a feather boa draped around the neck of a leather clad mannequin. It wasn't hard to think about sexy games with Josh as a partner. He oozed virility. Her exhibitionism foray had gotten her pretty hot, so her thoughts went immediately to a game that would get them naked and close.

"That's exactly the leather get-up you should wear."

She stepped closer to him and raised her eyelids in a suggestive flutter. "I vote for you in uniform." Leaning in, she pouted her lips. "Officer, is it necessary to frisk me? I'll never be such a bad girl again."

"Can't break the rules, Miss. I need you to bend over my car for a thorough search. Any resistance, and I will restrain you with my fuzzy pink handcuffs." He dangled said handcuffs and every desire to be naughty rose like a platoon inside her.

"We'd have fun with this game."

Instead of agreeing with her, Josh picked up a bottle and scanned the label. "This is interesting. How about we throw in an edible lotion. This one heats up." He flipped the bottle over. "Too expensive."

Focus on winning, not playing games, like he's obviously doing. "Good idea though. Let's look for a substitute at the dollar store. We'd better get over there."

Josh held the door for her.

The dollar store was two storefronts down in the L-shaped plaza, between a lingerie outlet and an art store.

Inside, at least ten aisles stretched out with everything imaginable. Josh stopped a young guy in a smock. "Do you sell sheriff badges?"

"Yep. Here I'll show you." He led the way to the toy section.

After Josh grabbed a star-shaped badge from a hook on the wall, they both stood scanning the floor-to-ceiling accessories for dress up possibilities. A native headdress, a princess tiara, a plastic hammer. Her mind lingered on the image of Josh dressed as a repairman having a look under her sink.

She glanced his way. Maybe she'd read him wrong. Even though they were pressed for time, there was no stress in his posture, no tension in his stance. His smile could be saying 'I want you', at least she could pretend it did which sent her deeper into fantasy roleplaying. *Let me be your fantasy.* Even just for a day.

He snatched the gold-painted tiara off the shelf and set it on her head. "After chopping wood all day, it's my good fortune to find a sleeping beauty in the forest. How shall I stir her desire enough to wake her and end the evil curse?"

"Please don't leave me for the dwarves." Adair imagined laying still, eyes closed, not knowing where Josh would touch her, what he might do. She forced her mind back to the race. "The tiara is a definite yes."

He grabbed a plastic wrench off the display. "Did you call a repairman? Need some help with your shower faucet?"

"Yes, and I've worked so hard hand-washing my lingerie, I'm awfully hot." She trailed her fingers across the low neckline of her dress, biting back a giggle. "I've been waiting for you all morning to take my shower."

His smile sizzled over her skin. "Show me where that shower is, and I'll get you in soap suds ASAP."

"Perhaps, I should hold your tool until you need it." She slid her fingers down his arm to his hand and over the wrench. "Oh, yeah, repairman could definitely work."

"What about teacher/student?" Adair suggested. "A little adult education? We could get some good student stickers for a prompt or a wooden ruler to correct misbehaving."

"Who wouldn't want to be the bad boy in your class?"

"In my sexual education class?"

"Teach us what women really want."

He was making her want to go home with him right now and play games. Scenarios she'd never consider in real life were an incredibly arousing fantasy with a partner like Josh. How many times had she said 'let's pretend' as a kid? Yet she'd stopped playing games years ago. "Trying to concentrate here. Okay, we have a badge for the sheriff, tiara for Sleeping Beauty, wrench for repairman, stickers for teacher."

"Are those handcuffs?" Josh said.

Her gaze followed him as he reached for a plastic set.

"Not pink and fuzzy, but I could find a purpose for these. How about guard falling for his prisoner."

"Or a prisoner seducing her guard for a key to the cell. Definitely take the handcuffs. I like to give up control, it's hot."

"You do? I'll have to remember that. What about this idea then? Do you think it's sexy to have complete control? What if the guy was an android, programmed to fulfill every one of your commands?"

That place in her tummy, the one way down low, gave an exquisite clench. Josh doing exactly what she wished? Would that be sexy? "Yes and yes. It would also help a women get what she desired from her partner, you know, if she was shy about asking. A game like that could really loosen a person up."

"Oh, yeah? What would you have me do first?"

"You mean after you cooked a candle-lit dinner and cleaned up the kitchen?"

He laughed at that. "Yes, after that. I can get a decent meal on the table under candle light."

She leaned in close and then said her next words in a whisper against the hollow under his ear. "I'd love to taste your culinary specialty. Afterwards, I'd ask you to remove my shoes. Then slip your hands under my dress and slide my tights down over my thighs, over my knees, over my calves and off the ends of my toes. Then I'd ask you to sit down beside me on the couch, take my feet in your lap, and . . ."

"Yes? Keep going."

"Give me a good foot massage."

His chest fell as he exhaled a slow breath. "That, Adair, would be my pleasure."

She sighed. "Guess we can't fit in a foot massage."

"Not at the moment."

As much as moments later would be the culminations of so many fantasies come true, she couldn't see past today.

"Back to the race," he said. "What about throwing some other stuff in like feathers for a tease and something edible, like remember those packets of colored sugar we'd eat as kids. Not as expensive as the stuff at Naughty and Nice, but a good substitute for selective sprinkling."

A sugary trail down low on his naked belly from hip to hip. Yes, that could work. She imagined his gaze, burning with anticipation, following her mouth as she nibbled up the sugar with little licks of her tongue. "I like it. Great idea."

"Okay, I'll look for something edible, you grab feathers."

Adair found the craft aisle and grabbed a small watercolor set too. Body painting?

Josh met her at the end of the aisle armed with three plastic colored straws filled with sugar candy. "Three for a dollar. We have twenty minutes left."

She held up the paint set. "Nude portrait for an artsy painter and her subject?"

"Or an artist and his canvas. After seeing you against that wall mural, I can think of a few strokes I'd like to paint."

Her nipples tightened from the way he looked at her like she was the most desirous woman this side of the Greenwich time line. Oh, what the heck. She pulled him into the aisle and backed him against a wall of kitchen items. Her hands moved to touch him, to run under his clothes, to learn every inch of his body while she could.

They kissed hungrily, to her delight. She soaked him in, never being more in tune with where a man's body touched hers. More than the crazy arousal that heated her blood, he was like the place she wanted to come home to after being away a long time. He was every bit as exciting as she'd imagined. The muscles in his arms were hard planes as she ran her fingers over him. Power turned her on. Relinquishing control to him? She bit his lip as her excitement ratcheted.

Oops.

Good grief. She opened her eyes as a customer edged around them. "I don't usually make out in house wares."

"Me neither. I've always preferred the motor oil aisle."

What was she doing dreaming of a future and painting in Josh? *Sorry about that little lie I told, Josh, the one that made you want to kill yourself. No hard feelings?* She swallowed the truth down hard, way down, all the way down to China. Surely she could keep it there for one day.

"We better get going," she said.

With twelve minutes left, they ran across the parking lot to a pizza restaurant. Open concept seating meant they could assess the entire dining room.

Adair did a quick scan of the tables and saw three or four couples on their own. Just as she decided who to approach, he took her hand and stepped into the middle of the dining room. "Excuse me ladies and gents, I'm sorry to interrupt your lunch, but I have a request to make. My lovely partner and I are participating in a dating race competition, and as one of our tasks, we must get a couple to play a romantic game by 5:00 today. If anyone can help us out, it'd be appreciated."

Adair held her breath while the patrons murmured. They had no time to find a willing couple elsewhere. It had been a mistake to get sidetracked by her resurrected crush on Josh. What were the chances, they'd find a willing—

"We'd love to help you out," came a woman's voice from behind. Adair turned to see a grey-haired couple pulling their jackets on, the kind of couple that adorned ads for active living, senior style. Well-dressed, good looking, trim.

Josh squeezed her hand and took a couple steps toward the couple. "Err, the game is pretty sexual, I'm not sure if it's appropriate—"

"Why's that?" With perfect posture and a gaze like steel, the man stared down Josh with eyes that said, you-think-you-can-teach-me-something? "Fifty-six years ago, my wife and I smuggled art out of a country at war. We've spelunked through caves in South America, we've climbed Kilimanjaro, so if you think you've devised a game to surprise us, lad, then bring it on."

Josh held up his palms in an I-surrender gesture as Adair laughed and handed the suave man the shopping bag.

"The rules are inside. It's a pretty simple game. Lots will depend on your imagination. When you've finished, if you'd send a text to the guy on the rules page with your score and comments, we could win this thing."

"Time is important," Adair stressed. "We're racing against deadlines."

"That's a problem." The woman shot Adair a smile that could have curled the toes on Michelangelo's David. "Lovemaking has never been a race to Sid. Good thing we've got two hours, we better get home, sweetheart. I want you with a bottle of Malbec on our wool rug pronto."

Adair stifled a gasp, and gave the woman a hug, liking her instantly.

"Oh wait, nearly forgot, we need a picture of you to send to the judges. Is that okay?"

"I've got no problem with that. Hold on a moment, I have an idea." Sid snatched a red rose from the centre of a table. He dipped his wife who arched her back with remarkable flexibility and let the rose brush her cleavage. The gaze between them was hot enough to melt ozone. The restaurant patrons cheered as Josh took the picture.

Adair caught the pleased look in his eye as his phone rang. The smile on his face fell as he read the message. "Detour. Heartbreak challenge. If this is anything like that elimination challenge, I'm just saying, there are lines I won't cross to win."

CHAPTER TEN

"Meet you outside." Josh let Adair thank the couple as he left the restaurant to wait for the next message.

Adair joined him on the sidewalk. "It's 2:25. We're five minutes ahead of schedule. So what's our next task?"

"The message says: Josh and Adair, you've been chosen to take this impromptu challenge. Another couple in the race has hit a roadblock that could prevent them from finishing. Your challenge is to help solve their problem. You've got twenty minutes to get this done."

"That's a relief. Doesn't sound like an elimination."

He agreed. Five minutes later, they reached Maple Avenue. He hadn't received any personal details of the heartbreak couple, so Josh wasn't sure who to look for. He slowed down and crept along the street while Adair did a visual search.

"There, up ahead, on my side," she said. "I recognize that woman from the race."

So did he. The woman he'd seen earlier, the one he'd thought would make a good partner, the woman with crimson highlights. At the moment, she looked like she'd choose a slow crawl through broken glass over running in a dating race.

Josh parked the car. "We have fifteen minutes to feel this out, find what the problem is, and get them back in the race." Three people stood arguing on the sidewalk. He approached feeling a bit like an ambulance chaser.

A guy in running gear wore a hip belt fitted with a water bottle and an attitude fit for a fight. "I've been cleaning up cat puke, Lauren, cat puke!"

Lauren looked like she wanted to scat up the nearest maple. Cardinal lips pressed tight together, eyes flitting between the two men. Her partner—Josh had to give him credit—was tucked up close to Lauren like a protector. It didn't escape his notice the guy had her lipstick on his neck. Wonder if it had escaped the jogger's.

He pulled Adair to a stop and whispered in her ear. "We have to get rid of the jogger fast."

Lauren caught sight of Josh. Both recognition and relief showed on her face as if Josh was a saviour. "You're from the race," she said.

Adair glanced at Josh. "Can we help . . . somehow?"

Silence.

Lauren's race partner asked, "Do you know a good vet?"

This unleashed the jogger's rage. "Or a fucking dry cleaner since my suit is covered in Lauren's cat's puke."

He turned his attention back to Lauren. "You slept with me last night, asked me to sit with your sick cat, so you could attend a conference." He turned to Lauren's partner and repeated. "That's what she said—a conference. You must be the keynote speaker."

Adair took a step closer to the jogger. "I know a great vet. I'll give you directions. Sounds like that cat needs help fast."

The who-the-hell-are-you look the jogger threw Adair was comical.

Lauren's partner winked at Josh and pursed his lips in a 'she's sizzling' gesture. "It's just a friendly little game, err . . ."

Lauren nodded her head toward the jogger, "Ryan, this is Charles, my partner in a contest I entered. I didn't tell you because—"

"Because you're a slut." Ryan finished for her. His voice cracked on slut.

That comment lit a fire under Charles. As the two men threatened to pound each other, Josh pieced the mess together. This wasn't about cat puke and a ruined suit. This was indeed about heartbreak. Josh would bet that Ryan thought he and Lauren were monogamous.

He looked at Adair and flicked his head toward the arguing couple—what should they do? Adair took a step back. "Not getting involved in their love life," she whispered.

The words now flinging back and forth between Lauren and Ryan were hauntingly familiar. Accusations and denials, truths and lies, shame and guilt. Erect a brick wall against feelings like that. That's what you do. You don't feel it.

"Why didn't you just tell me your feelings had changed," Ryan said. "Tell me you wanted to take a break, wanted someone else. But lie to me, Lauren?"

Both women on the sidewalk had trouble with the truth. What the hell was wrong with them?

"I don't know why I entered the race; for the prize money, for the excitement?" Lauren said. "I don't know. You and I were getting so close, so exclusive. I felt stifled, but at the same time, I . . . ."

"Try being honest, Lauren," Josh said, putting on his social worker hat. "If you don't want to lose him, say so. Sometimes you don't know what you want until you don't have it anymore." He turned his attention to Ryan. "This game is just a race for a prize, nothing to get excited about."

He knew their problems weren't a direct reflection of him, but the past loomed close to him today for some reason. Memories of the high school spring dance had been packed up and cast into the dark long ago. When he'd finally walked into the light, he'd done so by leaving that part of his life behind, all except for Sarah that is. There was no forgetting when it came to her.

Lauren and Ryan stopped yelling at each other.

"I've been thinking about you all day, Ryan," Lauren said. "We had to do silly tasks and well, no offense to Charles, but he's not nearly as creative as you are. I wanted to text you for ideas."

Charles looked at Adair. "She thinks my perfectionism stifles my creativity."

Adair gave him a sympathetic look and motioned that he should wipe the lipstick from his neck.

Lauren continued her confession to Ryan. "I shouldn't have lied. I don't want to lose you, but I want a few changes."

"Don't be scared to talk to me, baby. Come home with me now?"

"Yeah, have a great life, Lauren," Charles said, as he walked away. "I'm allergic to cats anyway, can't stand the little buggers."

While Lauren said goodbye to Charles, Adair sidestepped closer to Josh and spoke softly. "Glad they sorted it out, but do you think we'll lose points?"

"We salvaged a relationship, just not the one playing the game."

"Less competition for us."

"Yeah, and thanks for your help. If you'd moved one more step back, you'd have been part of that window display."

"It makes me queasy to bud into people's relationship issues."

Josh sent a message to their contact reporting that the relationship was on the mend. It wasn't his job to convey that Charles and Lauren would bow out. He couldn't help admiring Lauren. She admitted what she'd done and why, no covering up. What would have happened to him if he'd come clean thirteen years ago instead of letting people believe he'd tried to commit suicide?

And what about right now? Today. He'd told Adair he'd been in juvenile detention, but he'd not told her why. Would he feel absolved if he just said the words? *I drove a car drunk and nearly killed someone.* Or would he still feel the gut-eating shame?

He drove the thought from his head.

What was wrong with him today? Like he needed to take a road trip down memory lane. Pack a few bags of regret and resentment. Throw them in the trunk with a box of guilt.

Life was for living. In the present. No looking back. No looking forward.

That's how a happy life worked.

A text arrived. He read it to Adair. "Your next challenge awaits you at 710 Redford Road. Hope you've determined what your partner desires."

They ran back to Josh's car. He started the engine, not quite knowing what he desired. Adair had the most beautiful eyes he'd ever seen, and the things she did with those eyes were seductive as hell. Since she'd gotten wet, her ebony hair tumbled wildly over her shoulders and down her gorgeous back. With one touch of her coral lips, he was breathing in her passion and forgetting those lips had lied to him within five minutes of their meeting.

Like he'd never stretched the truth. Or was he making that concession because he couldn't get that topless image of her out of his head.

"Redford Road is west of here?" he asked.

"Yes, parallel to Maple. About five minutes." Adair buckled up. "I feel like I'm gathering data for a cheesy magazine article. So tell me, Josh Cohen, voted most ogled by a gazillion readers last month, what do men really desire?"

He smiled. He'd read an article like that a few months ago at his chiropractor's office and was surprised by the number of men who wanted an emotional connection with a woman. He wasn't abnormal at all. "I want an independent woman with an adventurous spirit who's excited about her life and about making every experience count. What about you, Adair? Who's your perfect man?"

"Impressive. You hardly paused. I like adventure, too. My perfect man is considerate, confident, and creative. A man who could spend all day making out. It's about the journey, not the destination."

"Has that changed since you were seventeen? Do you still have a competitive spirit?" Had she ever had a competitive spirit?

She looked down.

He was usually a decent judge of character. There was something incongruent about Adair. Something that had nothing to do with poor kayaking skills. Something he planned to solve.

Her fingers played with the zipper on the backpack sitting on her knee. Her thumb stroking the zipper tab in little circles.

"I guess I do, yes. I want to win this race. Turn right at the light up ahead. Okay, silly questions now. Favorite season."

"They're not going to ask questions like that. This is about romance. They'll ask us something like, does your partner like to be on the top or the bottom. So?"

"It really depends on the mood. It's sexy to be on top when I want to be in control. Otherwise, I like to see a man's arms when he's on top, see him use his muscles to keep his weight off me. That show of strength is crazy sexy."

Damn. He didn't expect her to answer that question. Interesting. Confidence was just as sexy as vulnerability. He liked a woman who didn't have to prove every minute she was his equal, one who could rely on his strength.

He caught the number on a lighting store they passed— 700. They were close enough, so he pulled the car into a parking space on the street.

"We're here," Adair said. "Bert's ice cream shop. I remember this place. They changed location."

Josh's hand froze on the key as he turned off the ignition and looked up. Bert's green and purple sign with the twirling ice cream cone sat like a sentinel on the sidewalk by the entrance to the store. A new location, a freshly painted logo, but exactly the same as it had been thirteen years ago.

The memories came back. Where Carly had accused him of cheating. On a Formica table, she'd thrown a picture of him taken at the library when he'd been pressed against another girl. Someone had hated him enough to take that picture and show it to Carly.

He remembered every detail, the yellow stain on the table, the chair legs scraping across the floor, the smell of bubblegum ice cream, and the black feeling, blacker than the darkest monsters from hell. He'd been a kid, he'd been overwhelmed, and he couldn't control his actions after that.

His phone rang catching his attention and turning his thoughts upside down. A familiar, crazy mix of irritation and guilt ran through him when he saw who was calling.

CHAPTER ELEVEN

Adair got out of the car and stood on the sidewalk waiting for Josh. Bert's ice cream shop was one of the mainstays of the town. She remembered when it first opened down the street from Crestfield High. It had become an after-school hangout.

What was he doing? She leaned down to peek in the window. His color seemed to have paled unless it was a trick of light. She opened the door.

"Everything okay?"

He still hadn't answered his phone. "Yes, I'll be right there. Sorry, just need a minute."

She closed the door and hurried to the ice cream shop. Inside, was not as she remembered. Too bad, would have been some nice nostalgia. It was now half the size and had no booths. A circus mural decorated the back wall, clown, elephant, tightrope walker: all smiles. Three table and chair sets, painted in primary colors, sat empty in the front. They must cater to a younger crowd now.

Josh had the phone. With no instructions, she couldn't get started on their next task. She turned back toward the door but stopped. She was being watched.

A man stood against the counter, holding her in an acute gaze. She couldn't look away and had the feeling he knew it. His presence filled all the space in the room.

Behind him, the clock on the wall read 3:10. Cripes! They had to hurry.

"Welcome. You must tell me your heart's desire." The guy had a voice as melodic as choral bells, although the way he drew the words like a hot caress over her ears was far from holy. Her insides trembled, piqued by that one word—desire. Josh immediately came to mind.

"Nothing." Her face flushed as she realized where her thoughts had been. The guy was obviously speaking about ice cream. "I'm participating in Race of Hearts today. Maybe you've heard of it. I've just lost my partner."

"That is unfortunate. You better find him, you'll need him for the next challenge, Adair, and time is running out. You don't want to be eliminated."

Goosebumps rose on her skin. "You know my name."

His full lips turned into a smile that seemed to hold a cauldron of secrets. "I have a list of all the contestants."

Oh. He probably had their next task. Glancing behind her for Josh, she lowered her voice. "Could you quickly explain the elimination challenge?"

"No, I couldn't do that." When he said nothing more, yet kept his sharp gaze on her, she shivered and looked toward the door.

"I'll get Josh and be right back."

By the time she reached the car, Josh was locking up. Color had returned to his cheeks.

"Is everything okay?"

"Yes, it's all good. Sorry about that. Let's get moving. We've got to make up time." He grabbed her hand and ran toward the ice cream shop. "I hope there's a cherry involved here. I'd like to drag one by its stem over parts of your body."

An erotic pulse shot through her again, along with a dose of relief. His smile looked eager. Whatever had unsettled him, he appeared to have handled it.

Her hand in his was sweet. He held the door open for her.

"Ah, you found him," said ice-cream man. "For your next task, Josh, you've received a message. Read the question privately and send the answer back to me without speaking it out loud. You have twenty seconds."

While Josh answered the text, ice-cream man turned his attention to Adair. "You must now decide how Josh will answer. This is a test of how well you know your partner. Best to keep in mind that people are often not who they appear to be, Adair."

This guy was odd.

His intense gaze was a suggestion his words should mean something to her. For a second, her breath stopped in her throat. Unless he was a mind reader, he couldn't know about her past.

Josh stared at her with a quizzical look. What was he thinking? She let go her breath and tried to look nonchalant.

"Perhaps you've found the answer to everything your heart desires in Josh," said ice-cream man. "Let's see. Here's your question, Adair. What is Josh's favourite ice cream?"

The question was so unexpected, her laugh came out like a snort. "Ice cream? I thought you'd ask a deeper question, about romance or relationships or soul desires."

"My answer is sent," said Josh. "Come on, baby, what kind of ice-cream guy am I?"

"I think you're a play-it-safe kind of man. Could even be vanilla or chocolate. You like kids and have a Disney ring tone, so perhaps you're a fan of cotton candy. Good grief, there are sherbets, too."

"Ten seconds, Adair," said ice-cream man.

Her gaze flew over the tubs of ice cream in the cooler.

"Seven seconds."

"I'm going to guess mocha almond fudge. You said you like coffee and who doesn't like fudge?"

With the ice cream scoop in one hand and a cup in the other, ice-cream man opened the freezer and dug into one of the pails.

"Good guess," said Josh. "My second favourite ice cream."

She read the label on the pail where the guy scooped. "Cookies and cream."

"Yep. I've been a cookies and cream man from way back."

"I'm a raspberry ripple girl myself, but you can talk me into cookies and cream."

"Good news, Adair, since this is yours." The guy dispensed a swirl of whipped cream over the top and stuck a spoon in the cup before handing it to Adair. "Your next task is to enjoy this ice cream, but not from the cup, from somewhere on Josh. Your choice where to spoon it. You have ten minutes to send a picture that excites the female judges."

As Adair reached for the cup, ice-cream man slipped something into her hand. Her breath caught in her throat when his lips rose in a dark smile that suggested he was way out of her league in the sin department.

Instinct caused her to jam whatever he'd given her into her pocket as she grabbed the cup off the counter and headed for the door.

"We're not doing this here?" Josh asked, a step behind her.

"Nope, we're going to need privacy for this shot."

"You're making me nervous."

"You'll have to be brave."

He laughed. "You do know ice cream is cold."

"Cold can be therapeutic." She opened the backdoor of the car.

"Yeah, but I don't need therapy."

"Just take off your shirt and get in the backseat."

He glanced up and down the street and then peeled his shirt over his head.

Wow. Her insides woke up with a glorious stretch and started to purr like a pussycat. Surely he could feel the heat that held her gaze to his shoulders, his chest, and when he turned, the muscle definition in his back. Josh Cohen was pretty fit for a social worker.

Once he'd climbed onto the backseat, he sprawled with his back against the door, his hand resting on the button of his shorts. The pose did insane things to every sexual nerve running under her suddenly sensitive skin.

She closed her mouth before she licked her lips. There was room for her on the seat between his legs, but not much.

Any second now, she would drag her gaze from his bare chest. Just five more seconds to take in the lines of his body, the light dusting of black hair, the rise of pecs, the taut abdomen. Like finely mastered art, except Rembrandt never painted pecs like these.

"How's this?" he asked. "Tell me you're not planning to fill my navel."

Her mind jumped a little further south. They'd been warned they needed to please the female judges. She pictured her brand new shop on Market St. with an eviction notice slapped on the window before it even had the chance to open. "Nope, not the navel. If we really want to win this you need to unzip."

"You're kidding."

"I did bare my fair breasts."

"Payback time, huh."

She flashed him a smile and checked her watch. "We have four minutes."

He unzipped. He didn't go commando. Inside his shorts were black briefs. Poised on the edge of the seat, mindful of the cup of ice cream clutched between her thighs, she leaned closer. "Lift up." She grabbed hold of his briefs, meaning to wiggle them down low, just expose a little bit more skin.

Josh Cohen's cock sprang free. He let go a sound between a whistle and a groan.

Sweet heaven. She had Josh Cohen naked. Her heart took off like a conga-drum. She glanced out the window to the sidewalk, to where anyone walking by could see this magnificent cock too. No turning back now. "I have never felt so naughty in all my life."

He craned his neck behind him to check the window. "I'm a fan of you being naughty, but not of sharing this with all of Stonewood Hills."

She couldn't stop now. Her thoughts turned giddy. "In for a penis, in for a pound. Is that how the saying goes? Let's go for bust, Josh."

A quick intake of his breath sounded when she wrapped her hand around his shaft.

His curse was cut short by three firm strokes. He was thick, hard and stealing the breath from her lungs.

I can't believe I'm doing this! She clenched her thighs tight to savour the desire that wanted nothing to do with deadlines or games or cramped quarters. *Keep your mind on the photo, on the race, on the prize.*

"Adair, you keep doing that, and I'm going to . . . forfeit."

"You are so freaking sexy, we're going to win this, Josh. You ready for ice cream?"

His eyebrows darted up. "Ice cream where?"

She shot him her most wicked smile, laid the cup on his belly, and scooped a spoon of the cream. "Hold still."

The muscles in his stomach couldn't be strung tighter. She pushed the cream off the spoon with her thumb onto his satiny, pink head. The dollop started to slide toward the edge.

"Oops." She poked it back, so it sat straight. "Is that good for you?"

A thoroughly masculine sound rumbled from his throat. "Good Lord, woman, good doesn't begin to describe what I'm thinking right now."

She was thinking a man had never looked more like dessert.

He gave her the phone. "You take the picture before I melt it."

"One more thing." She felt around in her pocket for the item ice-cream man had given her. In her hand was a small gold coin. "This picture is worth the big bucks." She set the coin carefully on top of her dollop of cream. "Don't move, don't even breathe."

She shifted her body away from the window to let in more sun and zoomed the camera in for a close up, wishing she could send herself one of these shots. No time for that. She handed back the phone for him to send in the picture.

Excitement shot like wildfire through her blood. She wondered if he felt the same mix of thrill and vulnerability she'd experienced when she'd bared her breasts.

She reached for a napkin, then hesitated. What was the likelihood she'd have Josh in this position again? She quickly removed the coin. As he focussed on his phone, she leaned down and took him into her mouth. So sweet, so cold, so full.

A strangled curse came from him and his fingers settled in her hair.

She swirled her tongue over his head, licking off all traces of cookies and cream, loving that she now knew the taste of him, loving the spontaneity, loving how bold she could be.

They were in the back seat of his car on Redford Road. This was the rush that incited bad girls.

Just one more minute. One more pull of her lips. One more slide of her tongue. One more blissful moan tugged from his throat.

So bad. She'd never been this intimate with a man she'd just met. Josh was different. Her desire for him was complex, deeper than physical attraction, deeper than a high school crush. Her desire was driven by a need to erase every harm she'd ever caused.

Her actions were not fueled by guilt. No, not that.

"Baby, that feels—"

Her panties were wet by the time his sentence ended in a groan. She stopped thinking about right and wrong. The thought that she could give him crazy pleasure sent her tongue swirling over his head. His rock hard, satiny skin was stretched so tight.

Deep down she ached to feel him push inside and fill her. Could she straddle him here? Quickly.

A muffled shriek sounded in her ear. Josh scraped against her teeth as he jerked himself away.

"Fuck." He yanked his pants up.

She'd gone too far. All to satisfy her—

Another curse—not Josh.

"—in the broad daylight. Phone the police."

Adair sucked in a breath so quickly it nearly choked her. When she spun in the seat, she saw two women standing beside the car slicing into her with gazes evil enough to annihilate. "Oh, shit."

"Let's get the hell out of Dodge." Josh's door flew open.

As she exited, she heard him shout over the roof of the car, "Sorry, ladies. Inappropriate, I know. My fault. Don't call the police. We're leaving."

As Adair switched to the front seat, she tried to avoid stepping on one of the women's toes, plastered to the window as she'd been. "I didn't know what else to do. Bert's Ice cream was out of bananas."

She didn't even get a hint of a smile for that.

"You're sick, you—"

Luckily the car door slammed on the rest.

The tires squealed as Josh pulled away. "Adair, you drive me wild." But not so wild that he didn't slow down. He turned left at the next intersection, then right before pulling over to the side of the curb. "I hope you're free after the race."

She hesitated. More than anything, she wanted Josh, all of him. Not just one day, she wanted more than that. A string of anxiety tightened in her chest. Any relationship with Josh was doomed. She pictured a distant day with them crazy in love. The day when he opened up, revealed his past and shared the heartache and desperation that nearly destroyed him in high school. Would she listen quietly, or would she admit she'd known all along who he was?

He reached for her hand and pulled her to him for a kiss. She melted into his lips. His kiss was passionate and playful.

Lips and tongue, fervor and hunger. He kissed with his whole being. Warm hands cupping her face, then his fingers moving rhythmically through her hair. His chest rose and fell against hers, his hips moving in a slow dance.

Hotter now, his hands slid over her hips, up her sides on the way to her breasts. She pressed a little closer, a little closer.

Whack! Her elbow hit the gearshift.

Pain vibrated up her arm. She nearly bit his lip. "Oh, man, that hurts."

"Sorry about that. It's been a while since I made out in a car."

Despite the pain radiating from her funny bone, she'd never been happier on a date. She'd known all those years ago she and Josh would be fireworks together. The crush that became a high school obsession had risen from Carly's many criticisms of him. Adair had not been Carly's best friend, had only spent a few months in that circle, but when Carly complained about Joshua applying for a fine art program, Adair was intrigued. The more she learned from Carly, the more Adair believed she was Josh's perfect match. Carly only wanted to be seen on the arm of the hottest guy in school.

Annalise, the Full Circle healer, said to look for synchronistic moments in your life. Adair and Josh had been paired together today for a reason. What better reason than a chance at love?

CHAPTER TWELVE

As they waited for their next task, Josh kissed Adair's elbow better. There were seventy-five minutes left in the race.

It had been a long time since he'd called a woman for a second date. Only once in his life, he'd met someone one he couldn't stop thinking about. At the time, he had no idea how rare those occurrences would be. He suspected Adair Ellis had a presence that would linger.

Any man would be attracted to her spectacular looks, her fun-loving nature, the hunger in her eyes, the things she did with that exquisite mouth. But there was something about Adair he couldn't quite identify, something he lacked in his life, something that made her stand out, something that made him want more of her.

He didn't need to be such a hardass when it came to her stretching the truth. There could be many reasons for her poor paddling today. He shouldn't have jumped to the conclusion she'd deliberately lied.

"You look like you're lost in thought," she said. "Strategizing?"

He sent her a look infused with exactly what was on his mind. "I was thinking of the prize at the end of the game."

"Me, too. Twenty-five thousand dollars can save my life."

"I was thinking about the weekend away with you—that prize."

A hint of skepticism tainted her smile. There it was again, a flicker behind her eyes, a hurt or a vulnerability.

"You don't like the idea?" he asked.

"No, I love the idea. It's just . . ."

He waited.

"It was a nice thing to say. Thank you."

"I meant it, Adair. I'd like to see more of you."

His phone buzzed. He pulled it out of his pocket, read the message and cursed under his breath. "We were late with the last one by three minutes."

"Oh no, what if we came in last? That elimination challenge. It's my fault. I got carried away. I'm sorry."

"Geez, don't be sorry. I'd forgo the winnings before trading out those minutes."

She turned to look out the window, but not before he saw the tension lines in her brow. "Hey," he said softly, reaching for her arm. Then he received another text. "Josh and Adair, with bonus points, you're now in 4th place."

Her relief was palpable. He'd never seen a smile hold so much promise. "We can win this," she said. "No, not can. We *will* win this. Right now, picture us on the podium accepting the prize."

Great attitude. He liked the way being with Adair made him feel energized. Lively and open, she was a woman who didn't hold back.

He suddenly saw himself through a new lens. When had he become a slave to his secrets? He should be living life for each experience, with enthusiasm, just like Adair. "What's the first thing you'll do with the prize money?"

When she turned in her seat to face him and slid her knee forward, his gaze flickered over her sexy thighs. Damn, even her skin glimmered with vitality.

"Nothing original—pay off some debts. I'm starting a new business." She touched the brim of her hat. "I make accessories, hats mostly. Cameron Duff bought the hat off my head last year when my cousin and I were in a Starbucks in Florida. My one brush with fame. We figured if they were good enough for her, we should start a business."

"Should I know who Cameron Duff is?"

"Well, she's a pretty famous designer who used to have her own reality show. She let me take a picture of her wearing my hat, so now I have it framed for my shop."

Creative and ambitious. Not scared to follow her life's dream. That thought needled him. He'd had a dream once. For a second, he remembered how time moved at warp-speed when he'd played around with graphic designs.

A new message arrived. "We have two more tasks to go. I'll read what was just sent. Travel to The Next Chapter Bookstore. Find David Matthews who will direct you to the romance section. There, you must choose a short scene to read aloud for an audience. You'll need three people to give you a score out of ten. Take a picture of your scores by 4:00."

He started the car and glanced at Adair before checking his mirrors. "You probably didn't have time for high school drama as well as competitive kayaking."

He caught her wince, but he didn't regret the poke. Adair was hiding something, and he'd bet it was something innocent.

"No, I've never done any acting."

That, he believed.

"But I'm not nervous. I'm trying to remember some of the books I've read. Foremost, we want to entertain our audience, make them feel good. Should we engage them with something comedic?"

"Or sexy?"

"We should keep it family rated." Adair made a few suggestions as they drove. Stonewood Hills had one of the last independent bookstores still standing. The store was a historical icon built from granite fieldstone scraped off the Canadian Shield by glaciers in the Pleistocene Epoch. Set on Lake Ontario, the town had been a ship building and wheat farming community a century ago. Now, merged with its neighbouring communities, it was a suburb of Toronto.

The worn floorboards creaked under their feet as they looked for David Matthews. Finding him nearby, David was a tall, balding man with a narrow face and long forehead dressed smart in a crisp, white shirt and navy blazer. He picked up the score cards from the counter. "Welcome to The Next Chapter. You're our third couple today. Seems the quest for true love is alive and well. The staff is enjoying this race immensely, and the store has never been busier, so there'll be many volunteers to judge your reading."

"Great, lead the way." Josh moved aside to let Adair go first. Again, her smile was full of life, full of exuberance, full of sensual promise. As she passed him, her fingers trailed across his lower back. Nice to be with a woman who didn't hesitate to touch.

The bookstore had a welcoming atmosphere with a small cafe off to the side and leather chairs where customers could sip lattes and read.

They walked past dozens of browsing people before reaching the back of the store. "Here you go," said David. "We have an extensive romance collection. It's the most popular section which bodes well for the world, don't you think?" His gaze passed over Adair.

"It bodes well for me, David," Josh said, before the bookseller started to drool. "We'll let you know when we've chosen a book."

"Very good, then. When you're ready, I'll make an announcement. We have a quiet alcove for the reading."

Josh chose a novel from the shelf, one with a gowned beauty held captive by a pirate, and leafed through the pages, reading a few sentences here and there. "I think we need a book we know something about."

"I have some ideas." Adair crouched in front of one bookshelf. "Great, they have it. I love this author. She's witty and writes snappy dialogue." She pulled out a book and flipped to the back jacket.

Adair described a scene about a heroine whose life had taken a nosedive. She believed one night of uninhibited, anonymous sex with a hot Italian guy would prove she was not the sexless woman her ex-husband thought. She read a few lines to Josh. The scene was a riot.

They asked David to round up their audience. It took no more than one minute after the announcement hit the speakers for them to draw a crowd.

Adair started them off in the point of view of the heroine. Josh smiled thinking she captured the character perfectly. The dialogue was internal at first with the character convincing herself she was indeed a vixen who would have this Italian stallion breathless and begging for more.

Josh didn't doubt Adair could play a vixen in the bedroom, but to portray this uncertain character, her body language was awkward and hesitant and hilarious. The small crowd laughed as she approached Josh with a sexy smile under worry lines that crinkled her forehead.

Josh played the confused Italian, a man obviously attracted to this beauty, but questioning her predilection for one-night stands.

One line Adair could not say without laughing. She had a low laugh, like a sensual tease in his ears. The audience must have thought so, too. No one could hear the phrase she was trying to spit out, but they laughed with her. Incredibly cute.

They finished to cheers. The first judge said they picked a scene fitting the occasion perfectly since all the competitors were essentially on blind dates. He gave them a perfect ten.

Josh put his hand on Adair's shoulder and whispered in her ear. "You were spectacular."

The next judge said well done, but she'd have appreciated some context before they'd started reading because it took her a while to get it, but she gave them a ten.

The last judge asked for a copy of the book, so David was happy. She gave them ten too. Josh took a picture of the three judges flashing their perfect scores overhead.

When Adair stood close beside him, he had a hard time dragging his gaze from her slender neck, from skin so smooth and clear, he was starting to think of her as a delicacy to be savored. The fresh and lightly floral fragrance she wore reminded him that spring was a great season. He never thought about flowery stuff like that. Whatever power she had over his senses, he wanted more. He wanted to breathe in her scent. He leaned closer.

"That was a riot. I think we did pretty good," Adair said.

"The high score is because of you. I'm going to come back and buy that book as a souvenir. I want you to read more to me."

Adair looked away and Josh was sure this time he didn't imagine the incongruity he saw behind her eyes.

CHAPTER THIRTEEN

Adair would love to read Josh a bedtime story every night for the next millennium. There was nothing she wanted more. And that sucked. There was no forgetting she'd been the one to send that life damaging tornado spinning through their lives. No forgetting the force of emotions.

Josh's presence had been like a radar beacon. Adair was doing her homework at the library when she'd spied him sitting nearby. She could almost feel the way her heart beat like a tattoo performed by a military drum line. He sat at a table twenty feet in front of her talking to another girl, their heads close together, backs to Adair.

When the girl touched her shoulder to his, jealously cut through Adair with the fierceness of a territorial wolf. She didn't stop to question the appropriateness of her feelings. She didn't care. When Josh slung his arm around that girl, Adair was incensed. When that girl laid her head on his shoulder, Adair wanted to chop it off.

A ridiculous over-reaction, she realized later.

She didn't want to remember what she'd done next.

There were millions of men in the world, and she needed to stop fixating on this one. Enjoy the day and get on with life. When his phone rang, she sighed with cowardly relief and leaned over to read what she thought was a message from their contact. When it registered that he'd received a personal call, she looked away, but not before she saw the caller ID—Sarah Beran.

"I have to take this call." He put the phone to his ear. "Hi, Sarah. How did the application go?"

Adair would have walked away, but people blocked them into the bookcases.

Josh paused, then said, "Sweetheart, I'll come over tomorrow and help you with it."

Adair finally broke free from the crowd. He'd called her sweetheart. The monster inside her woke up and climbed out of the cobwebs. The monster that wanted to take ownership of Josh Cohen's heart.

***

Josh shoved his cell in his pocket and caught up with Adair at the front door of the store. "Sorry about that. We got a message with good news. It's the last task and we've moved up to second place. We need to get over to Phantasy Photography, then get back to the clubhouse by 5:00."

Adair cheered and checked her watch. "Forty-five minutes. We better go."

Ten minutes later, they walked through the doors of the photography studio. His mind was half-stuck on Sarah. It was time for her to wake up and see their relationship was not working. He knew his guilt drove him to serve her every whim, he just didn't know how to step back without feeling like an ass.

The shopkeeper explained they needed to choose costumes and props from the store's wide selection. "What about saloon girl and cowboy. That's popular." She held up a red and black corset.

"What do you think, Josh?"

"Nah." Saloon girl was sexy, but it didn't suit Adair. She could pull off a more exotic guise than saloon girl. "Let's go for something uncommon."

"Pirates? Vampires?" suggested the proprietor. "The Bride of Frankenstein?"

"Anything else?" Josh crossed the shop and flipped through a rack of costumes.

"We don't have much time, Josh."

He stopped at an effervescent aqua and emerald shimmering corset. "Adair, you'd be a stunning mermaid with your affinity for the water."

She pursed her lips in a half smile and ran her fingers through her curls. "Under the sea, that's me."

"Love your curls. I'm glad you got dunked."

"I have a mermaid wig, but he's right, you have lovely curls," the shopkeeper said.

Adair grumbled and took the costume from Josh. "What about you? King Triton?"

"My mermaid to command?"

The shopkeeper headed for the men's rack. "I'll pull together a king of the sea costume."

With their hangers in hand, Adair and Josh were shown to the change rooms.

When Josh went to enter a room across from Adair, she stopped him. "Josh, I'd like to ask a question."

"Shoot."

"You're not dating someone, are you?"

"You overheard that phone call. No, I'm not dating Sarah. Far from it."

"In that case, would my king prefer to share a room?"

"My mermaid is well informed as to her king's preferences." The change room was a decent size. Josh locked the door. Mirrors hung on three walls with a counter across the back where a stool was tucked. Adair hung the costumes on a hook.

"For expedience sake," she said, "I think we should assist each other."

"As you wish. I am in need of a hand . . . your hand."

She slipped her hands under his shirt and ran them up his back, lifting his shirt up and over his head. His heart pumped faster as her gaze roamed over him.

"You have a tattoo," she said touching the symbol painted over his heart. "I hardly noticed it before."

"Wonder why."

A smiled curled her lips. With the tip of her finger she traced the three concentric circles. Inside the circles were three straight lines each topped with a dot. "What does it mean?"

"It's an Awen symbol from the Order of Bards, Ovates and Druids called the Triad of the Sunrises. To some people, the three lines relate to earth, sea and air or body, mind and spirit."

"To some people, but not you?"

"It's also said that Awen stands for the inspiration of the truth. The three foundations of Awen are the understanding of truth, the love of truth and the maintaining of truth. I learned that at a pivotal time in my life, so I did something permanent to remember it." Because his father hadn't let him tell the truth. Josh didn't know who'd started the rumor he'd tried to kill himself, but his father thought it less damaging than shaming the family with a possible negligent homicide charge.

But he wasn't going to share his sorry past with Adair.

"Oh." Her expression turned solemn and she stopped touching him.

He didn't like that. He took her hand and placed it back on his chest covered in his. "I also did it to piss off my dad in my rebellious stage. Now didn't you say something about helping me out of these clothes."

She leaned forward and kissed his chest just under his collarbone.

He took her chin to tilt her head and kiss her lips, hungry and fast. "I'm not sure how we're going to get this done on time."

"Do not fear, my liege, we have twenty minutes."

Another kiss and her fingers skimmed his waistband, opening his button and unzipping his shorts. He didn't want twenty minutes, he wanted twenty days.

He reached around her, found the zipper tab on the back of her dress and slid it down. She yanked his shorts off his hips and cupped his balls through his briefs.

Hot electric lust swam through his veins on a swift current to his groin. Sweet mercy. He loved her boldness.

Her breath breezed over his shoulder, long and deep and hot.

He unclasped her bra and groaned when she slipped inside his waistband and wrapped her hand around his shaft. "God, your hand feels good."

She nibbled his jaw and followed with a flick of her tongue. "I can't stop. I want you. Now."

He slid his hands over the curves of her hips and under her dress. To say he wanted her, too didn't nearly quantify his desire. "I'm yours."

She'd begun to stroke him slowly. The maddening pressure of her hand, warm and firm, sliding over his skin flooded his senses. He couldn't take a step away from her.

She kicked off her shoes without loosening her hold as he hiked her dress over her hips. He stripped her naked and slid his fingers between her legs. Slippery. He wanted her fast and hard. *Slow down. Don't act like a primate.*

She gave a little moan in his ear when he lay kisses on her breasts and flicked his tongue over her nipple. She was daring and beautiful. He was rock hard. He'd never been so turned on by a woman and didn't know how long he would last inside her. He picked her up, sat her on the counter, nudged her legs apart and dropped to a crouch.

Satiny pink folds, plump and inviting glistened in a nest of auburn curls. "You are beautiful, you know. You'd be a gorgeous redhead. Don't know why you dye your hair black."

Her legs snapped closed.

CHAPTER FOURTEEN

She'd forgotten she wanted to hide her true hair color from Josh. Hide every reminder of the person she'd once been, especially now she knew he'd tattooed the truth to his chest.

"Don't be shy, sweetheart." He kissed the top of her thigh.

She wasn't shy and she'd never been more excited.

She had Josh Cohen naked and between her legs. His nibbling across her hip was driving her wild.

The truth had no place in that change room.

Her mind closed the door on the past and zeroed in on the present. She wanted him. Firmer. Deeper.

When he nudged her thighs apart this time, she didn't resist. When the tip of his tongue flicked just where she wanted it, she gripped his skull. "Oh, yes, there." So easy now to forget about the race, forget about her debt. That sweet spot inside her clenched. Her breasts rose and fell as her breathing pulled from deep inside.

His tongue moved in long sensuous stokes. The erotic wave inside her was immediate and exquisite.

She fixed her gaze on the mirror across from them and watched the muscles in his back flex softly as he moved. Such a turn on.

His tongue swirled. Nothing softer.

A beautiful picture crouching in front of her. Lean, muscled and smooth skinned.

Oh, dear Lord. Another swirl. She bit her lip to silence her moan.

His butt, two firm mounds over muscular thighs. Insanely sexy.

He slipped a finger inside her. Her eyes fluttered closed as he slid over a whole new set of nerve endings. So good, so wet, so ready for him.

"Josh," her voice sounded ragged. She lowered it to a whisper. "I want you inside me."

His mouth closed over her pulsing nub and he sucked before lifting off.

She drew in a long breath, and a moan slipped out on her exhale. The backpack was squished up against the mirror. Josh grabbed it by the strap and yanked, digging inside and retrieving a condom. Two hours ago, she couldn't imagine using it.

Now, she waited breathlessly for him, wanting nothing more than to feel the intimate connection she'd imagined so many times.

"Comfortable?"

"Yes. Don't make me wait."

"Why? Tell me more." He rolled the condom in place and leaned forward to stop her words with his kiss. His mouth on hers heightened her excitement. She wrapped her legs around his hips. Her hand guided him inside as he devoured her with his mouth.

An incredible build up of sensation pounded her body with each thrust.

The look in his eyes, sweet, tender, much the way she'd thought he would be.

Wanted. Forbidden.

A wave of exquisite pleasure washed over those thoughts. Never, never had she felt anything as consuming. She gripped him with her legs as he sank into her over and over again. When her climax rolled through her, she ground her mouth against his shoulder to stifle her cry. A sexy, masculine groan sounded from his throat as he reached his peak, pumping against her, melding them together.

They collapsed into each other's arms, hearts pounding, her insides blissfully, sensually aglow. She didn't have the bones to support her. Breathless and boneless.

"Adair, you've drained me."

She laughed lightly against him. "I'm feeling much the same. I wish we had a few hours before we needed to move again."

"Me, too. I'd never tire of holding you in my arms."

Her sigh was audible. Why did he have to behave like the man of her dreams?

Emotion welled up inside her, embarrassingly so. She tamped it back down. There could only be this one time, she knew that. She'd hurt him so badly.

Why did sex with Josh have to be earth shattering? That kind of sex didn't make everything all better. It didn't make anything better. *Get back to reality before you rip open wounds that may never have healed.* "We should get moving. We lost ten minutes."

"Ten minutes of you rocking my world." Before she could move, he kissed her again. Too tender. *Move already!* But a force had hold of her, one that bound her to him because two parts had become one, because the universe was telling her she'd found her perfect mate.

As if. Her mind had fast-tracked back to teenage wonderstruck. *Stop being seventeen. Stop with the bigger-than-life crush on a guy she hardly knew. Stop filling in all the blanks with perfection. Stop making Josh into a dream come true when that dream is impossible.*

He shook out her dress from where it had landed on the floor in a clump and hung it on a hook. "We have to get you into this tail."

No piece of tail jokes please. She took the mermaid bikini top from him. Aquamarine sequins glittered under the light. His touch was still too tender as he helped her, lifting her hair off her shoulders, clasping, kissing, fingers gliding in soft caresses.

When she was dressed, he stood back to admire her. "You are the stuff of every mer-king's fantasies."

Her tail would clip on once she was positioned for the photo. For the moment she was adorned in a shimmering, aquamarine, sequinned bikini top and a skin-tight, thigh-length skirt.

"And you are a very naked king."

"Right, I'd better get dressed."

She didn't trust herself to touch him. Instead, she wished for something she could never have predicted. She wished Josh was less than ordinary.

She let her gaze travel over him.

Perhaps she was being hasty. Perhaps all would be blissful between them. Did she need to tell him what she'd done? She certainly didn't need to tell him anytime soon. If they fell in love, he'd see how she'd changed, how she'd never interfered in people's personal lives again. It was high school. Surely they'd get passed this.

Her stomach turned over. How would she get those words out? Words that paralyzed her? She would never tell him. That was the answer. People had secrets from each other. Right?

When he finished dressing, she sucked in a breath at the sight of him. Startlingly handsome didn't begin to describe. His costume looked medieval, an amethyst tunic over tight breeches, finished with a faux fur trimmed cape. "You look spectacular. You can be my king any day."

A knock sounded on their door. "You have less than five minutes for this picture. I'd suggest you get moving." The shopkeeper sounded impatient and no wonder.

Their lips parted in smiles. "How's the room look? We didn't destroy anything, did we?"

Josh did a quick scan of the room and opened the door for Adair.

They were ushered into a small studio where an under-the-sea background had been dropped behind a pink shell-shaped dais. The photographer, a thirty-something woman, in army boots and baggy pants, barked orders. "Help the mermaid onto her shell, sailor boy, so we can get her tail in place."

"Sailor boy? I'm king of the sea. You know what that means?"

"You've got barnacles growing on your . . . trident?"

"Okay, that's it. No caviar for you."

Fortunately, the photographer made up for personality with efficiency. They got their picture in time. The king of caviar looked as though he'd discovered buried treasure in the mermaid perched on a seashell.

"Nice bit of tail." One of their competitors poked his head into the studio before a cowgirl dragged him away.

"Picture is sent. We made it in time," said Josh. They changed back into their clothes and caught the shopkeeper's scorn at the front door.

"I've been asked to give you a message. You're supposed to go to the bar at The Cushion Club and ask for Donny. It's a bonus task, if you can rise to it." Her gaze bore into Josh. "It's the most difficult challenge yet. Perhaps one that will mean keeping your pants on." She snapped up a spray bottle of antiseptic and left them with her warning and disapproval.

CHAPTER FIFTEEN

Back at the Cushion Club, Josh and Adair were directed to the bar in the lounge where they were given their final task. When the bartender explained Josh and Adair must make each other a drink, Josh's chest constricted.

"That's it?" asked Adair, turning to Josh. "The woman at the photography studio worried us for nothing."

Josh's laugh sounded uncomfortable in his ears. "Yeah, payback for messing around in her shop."

"I'm trying to remember if we shared what our favourite mixed drink was."

"Too late, you can't ask that now," said the bartender. He placed an envelope on the counter with their names on it. "As soon as you've finished your drinks, open the envelope, decipher the message, and you're done. Take your time. The judges need another thirty minutes to review the results."

From the corner of his eye, Josh watched Adair survey the selection of bottles lining the shelves. She reached for a bottle of coconut rum, then crossed her arms over her chest, and surveyed some more.

He didn't know much about mixing drinks. His usual response in these situations was to confess he didn't drink, but that'd be taken as cheating now. He doubted their winning depended on his drinking the drink Adair put together, and he didn't want to disturb her anyway. She looked so damn cute.

When he'd started the race, the last outcome he imagined was him mixing a drink thinking he found not just a really good woman, but a woman who was really good for him, a woman he could even see growing old with.

He'd have to remember to thank Lydia for pushing him into the race.

Adair glanced his way. Under the brim of her orange hat, her eyes sparkled with that unique liveliness over a smile that could jumpstart the dead. His smile rose instantly as she reached for a different bottle. It didn't matter what she came up with since he didn't have a favourite drink.

She, on the other hand, probably did. He looked over the labels for something sweet yet complex remembering the layered shots he'd seen women drink. His gaze fell on a bottle of Crème de Cacao. Sounded good. What woman didn't like chocolate? He glanced her way again.

Orange. She looked great in orange. He knew about Grand Marnier. Chocolate and orange had to be good. Adair was a multi-faceted woman and one that generated heat. He scanned the bottles and decided on a maple whiskey to top it off.

She'd turned her back to him, working on the other side of the bar as he put his drink together. They met in the middle and laughed. Their drinks looked much the same.

"That looks pretty good." She took the drink he offered. "We're both thinking similar thoughts. Shooters, so we can drink them fast and win this."

He took the drink from her and let out his breath. Damn. Before today, it had been a long time since he'd thought about the reason he didn't drink. As designated driver, every time he delivered a friend home safe, he felt the decency he wished had always been his nature.

She clinked her glass to his. "I want to say, without sounding cheesy, that I already feel that I've won today after meeting you. Cheers to us."

Could he drink to that?

He watched as she tipped her glass back. His glass was smooth and small in his hand. Adair set hers on the bar and rested her hand on the envelope, waiting.

So many moments today provoked memories he thought were old news, but now he realized he'd never buried the past. He'd been manacled to it. The decisions he'd made in his seventeenth year still shaped the decisions he made in his thirtieth. Maybe he'd been going at it all wrong. Maybe the past wasn't meant to stay buried. Maybe it was time to stop being afraid.

"Tell me you're not afraid of my drink," Adair said.

He stared at the three layers. Her innocent comment cut deep. He'd never had a drinking problem, wouldn't be falling off the wagon. He'd stopped drinking because he'd been scared shitless. He swallowed hard, as if he'd been suddenly garroted by the past.

Now was the time to break free. "Cheers to us, Adair. To this day and to many more." He tipped the glass back. The burn of liquor filled his throat and nostrils.

"It's tequila, sweetened by a lemon liqueur."

"My new favourite." He set the glass down on the counter.

Adair tore the envelope open. "I'm excited. I don't know why, but I feel like something good is going to happen."

"It already did. We are going to win this. I want that weekend with you. Say yes to next weekend, even if we don't win."

***

Yes was the only thing Adair wanted to say. "No, I can't, not next weekend. I'll be at the Artisan's Marketplace in Toronto. I'm going to be crazy busy this week." The little voice inside her head grew legs and gave her a swift kick. "Rain check?"

"Until then, I'll imagine two days of decadent indulgence with a beautiful woman."

"That does sound good, although I'm not sure what beautiful woman you're imagining."

He leaned toward her and bit her neck. "Just read the instructions, beautiful."

Even after being doused in lake water, eyeliner obliterated, hairstyle destroyed, Adair felt beautiful. Josh made her feel like the most desired woman in the galaxy.

She peeked inside the envelope to see pieces of what could be a photograph. "Looks like a puzzle we have to put together." She dumped the contents on the counter. "I love puzzles."

"I don't mean to brag, but I won a puzzle competition in grade four." Josh started turning the pieces over. One side of the pieces had pictures and on the other side was a message. "We'll do the picture side? May be easier."

Josh pulled out the corner pieces. They worked quietly fitting pieces together. Adair worked on trees and Josh worked on what looked like a table.

When Adair put the pieces together along the top, she realized she had assembled the inside of a window that looked out into a forest. "Nice view. I thought maybe it was a picture of us taken somewhere today."

"I don't think so. I don't see orange anywhere in these pieces."

"Maybe it's one of the other contestants and another challenge. We have to find them before we can finish the race."

"Looks like a man and woman." Josh slid another piece into place. "See the legs, one is wearing a skirt."

Adair squinted even though she didn't have a problem with her vision. A sudden queasiness steamrolled over her bliss. But it couldn't be.

She could almost believe in a trick of light or hope she was suffering a bout of senility—almost—if not for the tension that rolled off Josh, or the deadly silence as he placed the last piece.

"That's me," he said. "From high school. It's the picture of me and Melinda Grant in the school library." He leaned closer. "The picture makes it look like we're making out, but we weren't. Her dog died. I gave her a hug and she wouldn't let go." He looked toward the bartender who was busy serving a customer at the other end. "What the fuck is going on here?"

Adair was going to throw up. Her stomach convulsed around the drink she'd just swallowed. A dense black fog invaded her mind. It couldn't be the same picture she snapped in the library thirteen years ago. The one with her message to Carly on the back.

Josh reached for a roll of tape that sat beside the cash register. "I don't remember what it said on the back." He tore off one long strip of tape and slapped it across the picture, then another and another until it was stable enough to turn over.

Adair watched the picture turn. Had she signed it? She couldn't remember. Time slowed giving her a moment to pluck the right words from her brain to stop him or to soothe him or to say goodbye. But she didn't do any of those things. She stood frozen by a revelation that could destroy every sweet moment of the day.

He read the message scrawled on the back. "Carly, sorry to be the one to tell you, but I saw Josh making out with Melinda. Did you two break up?" It was signed with the letter A.

He lifted his gaze and stared at Adair. "I never figured out who A was."

She stood frozen like a weather-ravaged stump staring into his perplexed eyes.

Back in high school, he'd not come back to classes after the breakup and no one seemed to know about the picture. All gossip was on his suicide attempt.

"It was a long time ago," she said. *Nothing good will come by dredging up the past.* She meant to express that thought, but the words stayed lodged in her throat. If she admitted the truth, she'd never again see that look of adoration in his eyes, never again feel that exquisite build of excitement rolling through her from his touch.

This was a man who so valued the truth, he'd tattooed it to his chest. And she couldn't tell it.

Why had she spent one second fantasizing about another date with Josh? It was never going to work, and he didn't really go for frizzy-haired, skinny women anyway. Men wanted women like her sister, the 'beautiful and smart' Ellis girl. Adair was blessed with creativity. Everyone said so. Creativity and a supreme talent for burying the truth.

Adair swallowed. "It's probably healthy to just let this go and forget—"

"Who left this photo here?" A vein in Josh's neck bulged as he waved the photo at the bartender, but the guy was still busy.

Someone knew. Someone wanted him to know. She turned her head and scanned the lounge. Fear pumped through her veins. Josh took a step away from her toward the bartender.

Annalise's words came back to her. *Acknowledging the feeling allows you to let it go.*

She could end this now and come clean to the person who mattered.

Another shot of fear made a cesspool of her belly.

Coming clean may add fuel to Josh's fire. This would all go away if she just ran.

Great plan. And then what?

She must think rationally and fast. Why was she so afraid?

Because he'd think she was a bad person.

Yet when she'd shared her secret with the emotional freedom group, no one had judged. Everyone made mistakes, that's what they'd said.

It was high school. Old news.

He deserved to know the truth.

She grabbed his arm. "It was me. I took the photo."

CHAPTER SIXTEEN

The neural connections in Josh's brain sluggishly processed Adair's confession—the photo taken thirteen years ago, the photo that led to Carly's accusations and the end of their relationship, the photo that led to the fury that had possessed him like a demon. The car. The speed. The crash.

The photo trembled in his hand as his throat closed, no longer with bewilderment, no longer with regret, no longer from the lie that had so brutally affected his life, but from Adair's admission—the new lie.

Her mouth opened and then closed.

"You took this picture? You knew who I was all this time and pretended you didn't."

"I . . . I never meant to hurt anyone. I was young, so young, with an overwhelming crush on you that felt like . . . like something desperate. It sounds ridiculous now, but I always wanted to make amends, somehow. I just didn't know how. I'm so sorry."

I always wanted to make amends. He knew all about trying to make amends. Amends were fucking impossible.

He'd never be released from that day. But now he knew who'd set it all in motion. Now he had a face, a name.

Adair.

"I'll send your apologies along to Sarah. She's the one whose life was ruined."

Adair reached for him, but he stepped back.

"We're always responsible for our actions, Adair, always. You tried to cover up yours. My parents tried to cover up mine, but sooner or later things like that resurface. Doesn't matter that you're sorry. As I see it, not much has changed. You lied thirteen years ago and you're still telling lies today." Each word had jagged edges that ruined his throat.

The intense, sexual connection between he and Adair from the moment they'd kissed had caught him off guard. No wonder. In a sick way they were connected.

She said something, a plea, an excuse, but he didn't have the stomach to listen.

His hands curled into fists at his sides.

He turned his back on her and cut across the lounge, across the lobby. His elbow whacked a guy as he passed, but he didn't apologize. The edge of his car keys dug into the palm of his hand as he crossed the parking lot.

Adair had known all day long. Every moment was one lie tossed on top of another.

His feet ate up the asphalt as he headed for his car. Inside, he slammed the door shut and started the engine. Anger pounded at his temples. He felt it and he embraced it.

The tires squealed when he turned onto the road to get out of this town, get out for good. Get far from mistakes that would always needle him.

He pressed his foot to the gas pedal.

His cell rang. He lifted his hip off the seat to reach for the phone in his pocket, pulled it free and saw the incoming call.

Fuck.

He'd never be free from Sarah either.

Don't answer. Never. Again. Sarah was a tether to the person he didn't want to be.

He glanced at his phone.

Ring.

Ring.

Ring.

Red streetlight. His heart jumped. He slammed his foot to the brake pedal. Tires screeched. Phone flew. Fingers bit the steering wheel.

The old woman's screams ripped through his head. Cursing, screeching, sobbing.

His car skidded to a stop just inside the intersection. Sweat flooded from his pores. He'd not heard that old lady scream in a decade.

His breath came out in pants as he looked left and right.

There was no screaming.

No old woman. No pedestrians.

Stop making yourself crazy. He took another breath, drew it in long and slow. Then out. He did it a few more times. On the next exhale he started to feel the panic easing. Breathe. Let it go.

He was over-reacting. As a matter of fact, he'd been over-reacting to things all day.

Must be a full moon in the sky because something had set him on edge.

Running wasn't the answer. It never was. He needed to turn the car around, go back to the club, and slay the demon that stood between him and a normal life.

A light flashed in his rear-view mirror. He looked up.

The police.

No fucking way.

Adrenalin blasted his heart all over again as he jammed the car into park.

He had alcohol in his blood, and he felt the buzz. Him. Josh Cohen. The guy who was supposed to know better was driving a car after downing a shot of tequila. Fear rose from its dank, dark den deep in his belly and snaked through his limbs.

Relax. Relax. Relax. He lowered his window and forced his jaw into a smile as the cop approached.

"Sorry, Officer, I guess I misjudged. Didn't mean to burn rubber."

The officer gave him one of those scornful looks meant for the very bad. "That's not why I pulled you over."

One drink. He'd had one drink in thirteen years.

"We got a call about an indecent exposure. Can I see your license and registration please?"

His throat went dry. What the hell would an indecent exposure charge do to his life? "I can explain that, Officer. I was in a dating race today, got a little frisky in the back seat, should never have let th—"

"License and registration please."

Josh handed them over and tried not to shit himself.

He'd be labelled a sexual deviant, a predator. Drunk driver was tame compared to this. Minutes dragged into forever as he watched his wretched life pass before his eyes and slither into a cesspool.

When the officer appeared back at his window, Josh stopped himself from wiping his palms on his pants, tried not to look like a nervous wreck.

"Hey, I noticed the sticker on your window from the Red Pine Wilderness program."

"Yeah, I'm a social worker. I do the treks when I have time, and I do some counseling." He swallowed hard. Shit lot of good his community service would do him now.

"My nephew went through that program, Brent Caulfield. He talked about the mentors a lot."

Recognition struck, thirteen-year-old gangly kid with over-sized ears. "I remember Brent. Good kid. How's he doing?"

"Great. Good program. Made a difference."

The office handed him back his papers. "Thank you for your cooperation. Remember the back seat of your car is public. Keep your zipper up and drive safe, Josh."

"Yes, I will, thanks. It won't happen again."

Once the officer reached his vehicle, Josh put his car in drive, and inched through the intersection, turned into a plaza, and parked the car. His heart still raced in his chest, too much for him to drive safe.

A burst of sunlight lit the car and glinted off something he saw from the corner of his eye. On the passenger side floor was a silver coin. He reached over, picked it up and realized it was the trinket Adair had put on top of the ice cream, on top of him.

He looked closer.

Across the top of the coin read St. Michael Children's Hospital–Wings Program. Engraved in the centre was a child on the summit of a mountain with the words— donations mean we soar.

Why would Bert's ice cream give away a silver coin from St. Michael's?

They wouldn't. It didn't make sense.

St. Michael's Hospital. The last time he'd seen the picture that Carly had thrown onto the table at Bert's ice cream, the same picture that had shown up today torn to pieces, had been at St. Michael's Hospital.

I never meant to hurt anyone. This time the words weren't his. This time he saw Adair's desperate plea in his mind's eye. She'd been just as shaken as him when that puzzle came together.

Now he knew it was Adair who had taken that picture. He'd always expected peace of mind with the realization, but at the moment his mind was far from peaceful.

Thirteen years ago, he'd thrown that picture into a trashcan at St. Michael's.

He wished the picture had stayed buried, wished it hadn't been Adair. He let his mind wander to how she'd felt in his arms, to what he'd felt with her that held promise. Then he let the reminisce go. To hold on was a betrayal to Sarah.

Sarah.

Then the pieces fell into place.

She'd orchestrated it all. The race. The picture. Adair.

CHAPTER SEVENTEEN

Adair stood silent in a room that buzzed with excitement. Who was Sarah? Why did she need an apology? How was her life ruined?

Her attention diverted to a woman whose laugh filled the posh Tudor Room. Someone was having a good time. Dark hardwood floors gleamed under a cathedral ceiling as the contestants waited for the winning announcement.

It was interesting to see the differences in the before and after, to see which couples had made a match, to see how one afternoon could change lives.

A guy with a pineapple tattooed on his arm winked at her, but she couldn't smile back.

The image of another tattoo filled her mind.

She'd been so right. His reaction was exactly as she'd predicted. He'd never get past her betrayal even though it was in high school.

She checked her watch. Where was Josh? He may not speak to her again, but surely he'd return to see if they'd won.

When the judges arrived and made their way to the front of the room, the contestants quietened down and waited for the announcement.

Adair said a silent prayer. *I know I've made mistakes in my life, but please, I need to pay my bills.*

One of the judges, a woman in red leather pants riding low enough to show a sparkle in her navel, took the microphone and thanked the contestants for participating in today's Race of Hearts. "I speak for all the judges when I say we've been impressed by the creativity shown today. Two teams were very close, but one of the couples in the romantic role-play took Sleeping Beauty to a whole new level."

Adair's nerves thinned to a razor edge. The older couple who'd agreed to play their game could have pushed an envelope or two.

The judge announced the second runner up. Wearing dejected smiles, two people collected their consolation prizes—movie passes.

Adair breathed with relief when she didn't place second.

"And now, the winners of the Cushion Club's Race of Hearts. Nina Chorley and Simon Warhol!"

The cheering droned in her head. Her debt flashed before her eyes and settled like debris in her tummy. What could she save? Her apartment or her shop? Her independence or her passion? Or would she lose both?

Stunned by sudden hopelessness, she stood in the room full of strangers, feeling as though the climb out of this pit was impossible.

A visual came to her of a picture of the steps from her Emotional Freedom classes. On one of the steps was gratitude. Maybe gratitude could help her climb from the pit.

I'm grateful for the free ticket that allowed me to run this race with Josh and maybe one day I'll even be grateful he discovered my secret.

The woman in red leather was speaking to an official from the contest. Adair poked her head out of the gloom and headed their way. "I need to talk to someone about a picture that was left at the bar."

"My name is Carrie. I'm the contest manager." Carrie was a well-put-together, fortyish woman with a whole-hearted smile until Adair explained what had happened.

"The picture was in pieces and left with the bartender?" Carrie's eyes narrowed defensively and Adair felt like bad press. "That task was not part of the contest. There were no clues to be left at the bar. The drinks were a courtesy while you waited for the announcement."

The bartender was finishing his shift when they reached the lounge. "I didn't see who dropped off the envelope, " he said. "It was left with a note explaining the drink challenge. I just followed the instructions." He pulled his car keys from his pocket and took a step to skirt around them. His gaze skimmed over Adair and settled on the door. "My grandmother's in the hospital. I've got to run."

The contest manager promised to look into it, but Adair didn't hold much hope.

She couldn't quell the taunting voice in her head, the one that said she deserved what she'd gotten today.

What goes around, comes around on the carousel of her life. She should know by now that her karmic destiny was a loveless void for the pain she'd caused.

If she was ever going to thwart destiny and overcome this once and for all, she couldn't avoid the scary, uncomfortable stuff like she'd done as a teenager. She needed answers to questions that would otherwise haunt her forever.

She and Josh hadn't exchanged any contact information. Her mind scrambled to figure out what to do next.

"Hey, sorry you didn't win." Her friend Jessie startled Adair with an exuberant hug. "I got here just in time for the announcement. What happened to your partner?" Jessie took a closer look at Adair. "Are you okay?"

Adair brought Jessie up to date.

"You've beaten yourself up over this for thirteen years," Jessie said. "You were a hormonal teenager. If you didn't have a regret or two or ten, you wouldn't be normal."

Jessie was right. Adair had carried this secret like an internal signpost that constantly flashed 'you are a terrible person, Adair Ellis.'

"I don't know who left that picture at the bar today. I don't know what happened to Josh after I gave Carly that picture. I don't know how Sarah figures in this. I don't know if she went to our high school. I don't know if Josh is more than just friends with Sarah. I don't know if . . ."

"What?"

If all day long she'd been using her secret as an excuse to walk away, so she didn't have to deal with the truth. "Never mind. I don't know."

"Why don't we take this one I-don't- know, at a time."

Adair took a breath. "Okay, how can we figure out who Sarah is?"

"How about Facebook? Why don't we look up Josh and see if we can find her there?" Jessie pulled out her phone. She didn't frown upon Adair for the terrible thing she'd done. Until today, Adair hadn't realized how self-deprecation had slipped so deeply under her skin. "His name is Joshua Cohen."

Jessie pulled up Joshua's profile and found his friends. "He doesn't have that many friends, only eighty-six." She began to scroll down the list. "There's a Sarah Dawes."

"I saw her last name, that wasn't it."

"Sarah Beran?"

"Yes!"

"She looks young." The picture was small, a blonde-haired girl with a narrow face and full lips. Adair couldn't help looking for a hint of Josh. "You don't think—"

"A daughter? You said Josh's parents wanted to cover up the truth. Maybe Carly was pregnant?"

"If she was, she hid it well," Adair said.

Luckily Sarah's profile was public. By her birthday, they determined she was sixteen, grew up in Stonewood Hills and went to Kittling Park high school.

"I think Josh would have mentioned if the girl phoning him today was his daughter." She did the math. "She'd have to have been conceived when he was fourteen, a bit young for fatherhood. The breakup happened when we were seventeen.

"Maybe she's family. A niece or cousin."

"If so, how did my breaking up Carly and Josh ruin Sarah's life?"

Pictures of Sarah striking different poses covered her profile. "Sarah's a bit of a duck face." Jessie scrolled down to read a couple comments. "She has a lot to say about the top model TV show."

Adair let her gaze follow one of the couples from the race who were leaving the club. They held hands as they walked to one of the parked cars. The guy pressed in close as the woman arched her back against the window, tilted her head, and kissed him.

"Look at this." Jessie drew her attention. "Sarah posted this picture last Thursday of her and Josh. Her comment is: Where's my man going to be on Saturday?"

Adair tilted the phone to see it better. "Doesn't sound like something a girl writes about her uncle."

"No. Sounds like Sarah has a thing for Joshua."

"It wouldn't be the first time a teenage girl fell for an older guy, especially one as sexy as all get out."

"I wonder if Josh ever looks at this stuff?" Jessie scrolled down as Adair read over her shoulder. "Sarah doesn't sound like she's suffering from a ruined life. Look at her interests: Windsor Modelling Agency, Scorpio Modelling Group, Model Photographers."

"And she's a cheerleader. Stop. Go back. What was that? She liked a breast augmentation site."

"She also keeps current on celebrity plastic surgeries and belongs to The Smithson Clinic group of plastic surgeons."

Jessie tilted her head to lean on Adair's bedraggled curls. "We are going to figure this out. You are not going to be pining after this guy for another decade. If he's as great as you think he is, then maybe you have to go get him."

"We have a cargo-hold of baggage between us. Besides, I have no idea how to find him. Don't know where he lives, don't know where he works."

Jessie had scrolled through Sarah's timeline. "We can find Sarah. She has cheerleading practice on Monday. If we pretend to be scouts from a modelling agency, we can ask her questions."

More lies. Adair's stomach twisted. She'd done a great job bottling up her tainted history. Her gut-wrenching troubles arose the day she'd put her nose where it had never belonged and here she was considering it again.

Time to make a choice. Tighten the cork on that bottle? Or unwind the damage and heal old wounds?

CHAPTER EIGHTEEN

On Monday, Adair spent the morning packaging up hats for the craft show and wondering if release from her financial noose would have made her happy. No matter how often she filled her mind with productive to-do's—and she had a ton of them—they didn't stick.

Her thoughts were constantly diverted by one all-encompassing issue: freedom.

Freedom from the accusing whispers in her mind when she'd tried to sleep. Guilt-driven whispers that kept her stuck to the belief she was a terrible person.

To make matters worse, she'd now compounded her emotional turmoil by wanting Josh in a bad way. It would be easier to deny the law of attraction between the moon and the earth. Never had she experienced such a connection, a chemistry, a force inside that pulled at her now, even when she stood alone in her shop.

Where had she left the packing tape? Her new shop looked like the post office at Christmas time. Good thing she had three weeks until her grand opening. *Yes, keep believing there's going to be a grand opening.* To make room, she pushed four stacked boxes against the back wall.

Did she have enough stock for the craft show? Her stomach tensed as she thought about selling her hats to customers face to face, creations she'd toiled over, pieces that said this is who I am. A much different experience than selling hats over the Internet. What if no one liked her?

Josh had liked her.

Well, until her secret had exploded with slightly less force than an H-bomb.

She gazed out her front window and let a different memory slip in. The feel of his fingers sliding through her hair, the tenderness when he placed a flower behind her ear, the gallantry that flared in him for her honor, and the most poignant of all—the way he'd looked at her with awe.

A sigh rose and blew through her lips. She closed her eyes and let the memories float into her thoughts.

Her cell phone rang. The Lion Sleeps Tonight—a text from Jessie.

She thought of Josh's ring tone and wondered what it said about them that both their rings revolved around the king of the jungle.

Enough.

Adair grabbed her purse and locked up the shop on her way out.

At 3:00, she met Jessie at the front door of the high school where kids streamed out from every door in the building.

It didn't take long to find the cheerleaders. The day was sunshiny and warm with practice taking place outside on the football field. Once they spotted Sarah, Jessie and Adair sat in the bleachers.

"I wonder if Sarah's parents know how public her Facebook is," said Adair. "Look how easily we found her. This is really dangerous."

"I was thinking the same thing." Jessie's hand lay flat on a folder from MacPherson Modelling Agency.

"This doesn't feel right," Adair said.

"There's no other way. Someone set you up with that picture. You deserve to know how Josh's breakup affected this girl's life. Looks like practice is over, let's go."

As she hung back, Adair's solar plexus constricted over the deception. From the day she'd ruined Josh's life, she'd vowed not to tell another lie. She didn't embellish. She didn't gossip. She didn't give unsolicited opinions. Yet here she was acting like a stalker.

But she meant no harm. The contrary in fact. If her actions had hurt this girl then she should at least try to make amends.

Jessie was ten steps ahead, approaching Sarah as she and a friend cut away from the rest of the girls. Adair tightened the lid on her discomfort and caught up to Jessie.

"Excuse me, ladies," Jessie said. "Do you have a moment to answer a couple questions? We're doing a little scouting for MacPherson Modelling Agency."

They couldn't have had a better cover story. Sarah's pretty face lit up like Times Square on New Year's Eve. She strutted catwalk-like steps toward them and smoothed her blonde streaked hair.

"My mom would never let me be a model," said Sarah's friend. "She thinks it's not healthy and emphasizes how you look instead of who you are." She turned to Sarah. "She's not as cool as your mom."

Sarah looked over to the parking lot. "My mom's waiting, so I only have a minute. I did an ad last year for a cookie mix. But I'm too old now for kid's stuff. I'm ready to model clothing or hair or makeup." She jutted out her hip and flipped her backpack over her shoulder.

Adair suppressed a smile and studied Sarah. There was something familiar about her, although Adair couldn't think from where.

"How was your last photo shoot?" Jessie asked. "Were you nervous? Are you comfortable in front of the camera?"

Sarah showed her perfect, white teeth. "Nervous? No, not at all. The photographer said I'm a natural. The camera loves me."

Adair wished she'd had Sarah's confidence as a teenager. Never would she have considered herself model worthy.

Jessie wrote down Sarah's response on their pseudo questionnaire making them look pseudo official. "Can you tell us what led you to modelling? As a young child, was it something you always wanted to do?"

Sarah stiffened. A frown wavered in the corner of her mouth. "My mother says I was posing in the crib. She had me young, so her modelling career never got off the ground."

"Your mother must be your biggest supporter," Jessie said.

"Probably, yes."

"Posing in the crib. You do sound like a natural. Did you model as a child?"

"I would have, but I couldn't. I was in the hospital a lot, but I'm all good now. I can work anytime. My mom will even home school me if necessary."

"It's not necessary," Adair said. "Hospitals aren't fun places for kids. That must have been difficult." Adair paused hoping Sarah would elaborate. She took a moment to scan Sarah from her spiral curls pulled into a ponytail to her clean, white sneakers. Sarah wasn't as tall as Adair at five foot seven, and she didn't have what Adair considered the classic model's body—thin boned, tall and emaciated. She did, however, know how to strike a pose.

"Would you ever consider cosmetic surgery?" Adair was pretty sure a reputable modelling agency wouldn't ask a teenager this question, but she wanted to know if the breast enhancement was something Sarah was seriously considering.

Sarah's friend bounced up and down on her heels and laughed. "Another thing my mom would never let me do."

"It's different for me," said Sarah. "I had to have surgery anyway. My mom says if God didn't expect us to improve, He wouldn't have made plastic surgeons. Attractive people get what they want in life."

Adair started to get a bad feeling about Sarah and her model-crazy-mommy-mentor. "Plastic surgery is expensive, no?"

"So is skiing and sailing and hockey and all the other things parents spend money on for their kids. I'm following my dream, and I'll do whatever it takes to make it happen.

Trudy Holmes had her nose and chin done when she was sixteen."

Adair had no idea who Trudy Holmes was, but she was horrified at the thought of sixteen year-old girls undergoing plastic surgery in the quest for prototypical perfection.

Jessie shot Adair an alarmed look that confirmed what Adair had been thinking. "Your chin and nose look perfect to me just the way they are."

They still hadn't learned anything about Sarah's relationship with Josh. "I can see you're dedicated. Modelling is a huge time commitment. Parents need to work and we don't like to see other family members neglected while our young models pursue their careers. Besides your mother, is there anyone else you can count on to be with you at photo shoots?"

Again, more grins from Sarah's friend followed by a sigh. "Only the hottest guy on the planet."

Sarah's smile could have lit up a black hole. "My boyfriend Josh. He'll do anything for me. Night or day, no matter how much time it takes or how much it costs."

"She's got that right," said the friend. "He's so awesome."

Pay dirt. Adair forced a smile. "It must be nice to have such a devoted boyfriend. Where did you meet? Does he go to your school?"

Sarah rolled her eyes. "I'm not into high school boys."

"Yeah, Sarah, for sure, and he'll get over you being a kid."

Sarah's eyes zeroed in on her friend like a heat-seeking missile. "I'm not a kid and he doesn't think of me that way anymore. You just wish you were pretty enough to get a man not a boy."

"It helps when the man owes you."

"You wish it was that. Josh feels good when he helps me, he says so all the time."

Jessie and Adair exchanged looks. What was going on between Josh and Sarah?

"I gotta go now," said Sarah. "Do you want my name?"

"No. Don't ever give your name to strangers," Jessie said. "Have a nice day, girls."

Sarah turned and took a step away.

"Sarah," Adair called after her. "Why does Josh owe you? What happened?"

Adair hardly dared to breathe as Sarah paused to consider. "I never said he owes me anything. It's my grandma who says that. She's the one who causes all the trouble between us."

A horn honked from the parking lot and Sarah looked that way. "I'm going to be late. Thanks for thinking of me for your agency."

"What do you think?" Jessie asked Adair once they stood alone.

"I don't know. Josh works with children with disabilities. Sarah said she was in the hospital a lot as a kid, so maybe they met through his work."

"That makes sense. But it still doesn't explain why Sarah's grandmother thinks Josh owes her." They started walking across the field to the parking lot.

"Or how my breaking up Josh and Carly ruined Sarah's life. Besides, she seems to be doing okay."

"Maybe you misunderstood Josh. How could you have had anything to do with that girl's life?"

"I don't know. You're probably right."

All they'd accomplished with this ruse was to heap another pile of unanswered questions on the compost of high school angst. And for what? Once again she was obsessed with Josh Cohen.

Get on with saving the pieces of your own life. "I can't waste any more time on this. Regardless of how my secret came out, it's over now. It's time to forget Josh and move on. I have too much at stake right now. Can you help me pick up a display stand for the Artisan show?"

The corners of Jessie's mouth turned down a touch. "Yes, I can. Listen, I won't bring this up again, if it's what you really want, but you say Josh's name like you want to hold on. Perhaps he's the one for you, perhaps not. But whatever you choose to do, believe you're worthy of the best man out there."

Adair hugged her friend. When she thought of the pain in Josh's eyes, she knew she had to give up on him. Every time he looked at her, he'd be reminded of why he'd wanted to end his life. She couldn't stand knowing he carried that association to her.

As they waited for a van to crawl past and join the line of cars exiting the parking lot, Adair's attention was diverted by the blonde girl sitting in the passenger seat. *Go on, Sarah, drive out of my life forever.*

The woman driving the van was also blonde.

A shiver raised gooseflesh on Adair's arms. "Good grief! I've met that woman. The one driving the van—Sarah's mother."

"What? Where?"

"Of course! Why didn't I think of her?" But the van had pulled ahead.

CHAPTER NINETEEN

Josh parked his car in front of the red, brick townhouse and walked up the six steps to the front door.

It was 7:00 on a Thursday evening and since there was a red Civic in the driveway, he figured the Beran family was home. Sarah answered the door.

"Josh! I didn't know you were coming over." She pushed her hair back from her face. "I played tennis today, and I didn't have a chance to shower yet."

He bit back his usual greeting, 'there's my girl' and instead asked her about school, knowing that conversation would be brief. Lately, when she was with her friends, she'd been acting strange around him, insinuating that he played an intimate role in her life. This had to stop.

They walked down the hall into the kitchen where they usually hung out since the room opened into a living area. It was a pretty kitchen, he guessed, bright with light colors. It had made him feel comfortable right from the start, like nothing was that bad with sunny yellow walls and cupboards painted the color of a robin's egg.

"I'm here to talk to your mother. She home?"

"She just came home from Grandma's. Mom!" Sarah yelled. "Josh is here." She turned to him. "Do you want something to drink?"

Tequila, double. "No, I'm good."

From his spot leaning against the counter, he watched Lydia come down the stairs. She didn't look at him, so he figured she knew why he was there.

"Sarah, go upstairs and do your homework. Josh and I need to talk privately."

"I'll get started on my social justice essay," Sarah said. "I hope you can look it over for me later, Josh."

"Give your mom and I a few minutes, please."

When Sarah ran up the stairs, Lydia plugged in the kettle and then stood back, she wrapped her arms around herself and finally looked him in the eye.

She looked tired which didn't surprise him. Lydia's mother could suck the energy from a rock. Lydia may have had some tough breaks in her life, the worst one Josh's doing, but that didn't excuse what had happened during Race of Hearts. He had to remember that and not let her do the usual and play to his guilt.

"Now you know," she said.

Yes, now he knew and surprisingly it had helped to hear Adair's side of the story and even more so, to hear her say she was sorry. "It was a lousy way to find out."

"Sometimes life is lousy." She opened a cupboard door and removed a box of tea. "Want some chai?"

"No, Lydia, I don't want chai. I want you to explain how you found out Adair took that picture. Explain the dramatics, the sabotage and whatever is wrong with you that made you think it was okay to hurt her like that. She was a teenager when it happened, not much older than Sarah is now."

Lydia told him about being at some workshop with Adair where she shared the story of how she broke up a couple in high school, him and Carly, and felt guilty for being responsible for Josh trying to commit suicide.

"So you thought the sane thing to do was let her believe the suicide attempt was true and plot an evil revenge."

She poured hot water into a mug and dipped in the tea bag. "Don't make it sound like a cartoon caper. Everyone was coddling her, trivializing what she'd done because she'd been young, as if it didn't matter that Sarah had to fight for her life and spend years in surgeries, that my mother had nightmares for a decade, that I didn't suffer, don't suffer every single day when my mother reminds me that I wasn't with Sarah when it happened—that I didn't hear the screech of the tires, the crash, the stroller scraping against the pavement, that I didn't see my daughter mangled by the car. It seems like every day, I pay for your mistake, for Adair's mistake, and I couldn't stand the thought of her being forgiven without paying a price. It's not fair."

God. His stomach hit the floor. He was so sorry. He'd been paying too, for thirteen years. Time served in juvenile detention had not come close to clearing the debt he owed, but sometimes he forgot how bad it had been for Lydia.

"You lashed out at Adair and me because you're hurting. Your mom lashes out at you because she's hurting. That needs to be healed. I've had some counselling. Adair's getting help with this. You and your mom need help, too."

She started to speak, but she stopped, then her arms seemed to fold herself into the smallest package. "I just want to stop feeling like a bad person."

No kidding. Didn't they all. "Then forgive yourself for not being there that day."

Lydia let go of herself and reached for her mug. "Adair's paid a price now. How did she look when she saw that picture?"

"Lydia, stop." He wanted to say more, tell her that if she could look at Adair with compassion instead of bitterness and blame . . .

"Guess it surprised you too," Lydia interrupted his thoughts. "You didn't know I'd taken it from the garbage that day in the hospital, but we both knew that whoever took that picture needed to be held accountable. Remember how frantic you were?"

He remembered. While Sarah lay comatose in a hospital bed, he'd shown that picture to Lydia as if it absolved him because Sarah wouldn't have been hurt if Adair hadn't taken that picture. But that wasn't true at all. The accident had been his fault, his alone. He'd been furious, he'd been drinking, and he'd driven his car through a red light and hit a little girl in a stroller pushed by her grandmother.

"I'm not upset with you, Josh. You've been so good to Sarah over the years, but Adair needed to suffer a consequence. She needed to lose something she'd once loved and that something was you."

***

Josh left Lydia's house feeling like shit. The righteous look in her eyes and the impassive way she'd justified her actions turned his stomach. He'd never believed in an eye-for-an-eye.

Over the next couple days, he thought a lot about Lydia's need for retribution and the part he played in filling that need. He wasn't so different from her—they were both shackled to the past.

At work on Wednesday afternoon, a message arrived in his inbox from Lydia. *"Josh, Sarah has an emergency on Saturday morning. I have an appointment, and she needs to get to her gymnastics competition. Please pick her up at 8 AM."*

Staring at the words, he let go a soft snort. She didn't ask any more, she assumed he'd do it, even after the stunt she'd pulled.

Walking away from Race of Hearts had been the best thing he'd done. He'd also walked away from the belief that handing the contest winnings over to Sarah would save his soul. There'd never be enough money to buy back his self-respect. He'd been doing everything he could to compensate for the suffering he'd caused, but he'd not done the one thing he most needed to do—give himself some slack. And compassion.

He threw the rest of the samosa he'd been eating into the garbage and hit reply.

Guilt rose in his gut, but for the first time, he didn't let it rule him. *"Lydia, I'm busy Saturday morning. Wish Sarah good luck from me."*

Despite the temptation to backspace, he hit send. Done.
It was time to stop feeling ashamed.

If only he knew how. He stared out his office window overlooking the skyscraper city, but didn't see much of anything.

He'd become a guy who played it safe to the point of stagnation. A guy who rarely spent time on his own happiness. A guy who maybe didn't even feel he deserved to be loved.

He not only set the bar high in his expectations of himself, but of others too.

Last weekend, Adair didn't measure up, so he'd written her off.

Now, he missed her.

She reminded him he used to be a different guy. She was fun, daring, imaginative, quick-witted and sexy as hell. And she wasn't afraid to take a risk.

He'd been like that once.

Unlike him, Adair hadn't run away—she'd told the truth. Now that he wasn't being a dick, he understood why she'd not admitted who she was from the start. Hell, he didn't tell anyone he'd nearly killed a little girl.

It was time to acknowledge the past had changed him for the better. He'd come out of juvenile detention determined never to go back, and he'd dedicated his life to helping others. And it was time to get off his high horse and do something about his future.

He picked up the phone and connected with his contact at Teen Help. "Hey, Denise, I'd like to talk to you about a speaking proposal."

"I'm listening. What's the topic?"

If he said it out loud, told his dark secret to the world, then maybe the shame would go away for good. "I want to talk to teenagers about drunk driving."

CHAPTER TWENTY

Adair stood at her booth at the Artisan's Marketplace surprised by how anticlimactic this moment was turning out to be. Her mom had offered to help set up, thinking Adair had been quiet that week because her cousin Elaine was not sharing the event. Her cousin's death was part of her melancholy, but a smaller part now.

A couple days ago, she'd gone to her emotional freedom class planning to confront Sarah's mother. But Lydia hadn't attended, which figured. A friend of Lydia's said she wouldn't be coming back.

Adair didn't tell the group what had happened. As painful as Race of Hearts had been, she finally felt liberated from the past. She'd told Josh the truth and now understood the adage, the truth will set you free.

As much as she hated confrontation, Adair drove to her uncle's home and spoke to him about the money she'd lent his daughter, Elaine. Adair had rent to pay and couldn't keep Elaine's secret any longer. That much, she'd learned.

Her uncle was a hot-tempered miser who people avoided, so asking him for money when he was grieving the loss of his daughter nearly cemented the request in her throat.

Until she envisioned Josh's tattoo and what it symbolized—the truth. Her heart beat loudly in her ears, and she stammered at first, but her words came out. "Uncle Dan, before she died, Elaine owed me ten-thousand dollars. I'm in desperate need of that money because I'm going to open a shop on Market Street, the Jolly Hatter."

She could have stopped there, but she didn't. She told Uncle Dan that Elaine had been saving her money to quit her job and focus full-time on their business.

She didn't tell him that Elaine had kept this secret from her father because he was a brute who opposed Elaine's creative endeavors. At the moment, he wasn't acting like a brute, but was softer, quieter, and smaller than she'd ever seen him.

Adair walked away from the meeting with Elaine's debt paid.

The truth worked.

On the way home, she made another decision—no more hiding her true self. She stopped at the drugstore and instead of buying her usual shade of jet black hair color, she bought one package of red hot.

As she stood under the shower watching the dye rinse out of her hair, she thought it symbolic. The past was where it belonged—down the drain.

Now, as she started to unpack her stock, she was optimistic. The curtained booth, one of the smallest sizes at the Artisan Marketplace was on the second floor down a long hallway designated to fashion. She'd brought four custom racks from her store and hoped her space would compete aesthetically with those in her surroundings.

Her mother had touched a nerve. Adair did want to share this achievement with someone. It just hadn't been her mom.

She blew a breath in a puff through her lips and sliced open a carton. One day, she'd find a good man to share the big things and the little things.

Her design was to group the hats by color so the booth would look like a rainbow. She glanced at the sketch on top of the box beside her.

The yellow hats were next to be placed. Where had she put her scissors? As she scanned her booth, a man heading down the hallway caught her attention. She looked away, whipped her back to him, and moved a carton to the floor.

Good grief! What was he doing here?

She spied the metallic gleam of a scissor handle and reached down to retrieve them, praying she'd been mistaken.

A few moments later she heard a voice. "You don't know where I can get hats, do you? I have to buy Christmas gifts for seven cousins, all girls."

She stood and turned to face Josh. Heat rose to her face. She internally cursed herself for feeling humiliated.

He stood there quietly, staring. "You changed your hair. I like it."

That's right. No more hiding from the young girl she'd been. She touched a curl. "Seven cousins, huh. You buy them all Christmas gifts?"

He took one of the orange hats off the rack and held it, his gaze on her. "I will this year. Your hats are spectacular. I'll get big points for this."

Her heart started to do somersaults up her throat. Look anywhere but in his eyes. She clutched her scissors and used the pointy part to tear open another box. "All hats are made from a lightweight weave that provides 95.8% blockage against UV rays, but feels cool to wear. They are fitted with a headband to remove moisture from the skin. The wide brim provides shade and further protection." She was well into her ramble. "They come in a rainbow of colors to flatter every skin tone and hair color, but I don't have them all unpacked yet, so just give me a moment—" Words died when she poked herself with the scissors. She sucked in a breath.

Blood trickled out of the hole in her finger as if she couldn't keep anything inside any longer.

"I'm going to lose points if there's blood on those hats. Give me your finger, Adair."

He had a tissue. She let him wrap it around her finger and press it tight to staunch the trickle.

"Do you always get a six-month jump on your Christmas shopping?"

"Well . . . no, not always. Okay, not ever." He hesitated and it felt as though every movement in the convention centre ceased when his fingers brushed against the palm of her hand. "I owe you an apology. My reaction to that picture from high school was knee jerk, mostly me being a jerk, and I'm sorry for that."

"Are you going to tell me what happened to Sarah?"

"I don't tell anyone what happened to Sarah. My father drilled that into me. He meant it as a protective gesture, but secrets like that eat away a person's soul."

"Yes, I know." She slipped her hand out of his grip. "Listen, I don't want to open any wounds. Let's leave the past in the past."

"No, that's not what I meant. I won't take a chance you blame yourself for any of this." His gaze swept the aisle beside her booth before settling back on Adair. "I had the truth inked into my skin, but I don't talk about what happened that day, what I did."

She went perfectly still.

"I was having a few beers with friends in Kew Park when I got a call from Carly. She was upset, wanted to meet at Bert's Ice Cream. She was crazy mad, accused me of cheating. We had a pretty ugly argument."

Adair knew exactly how angry Carly had been. Adair had unleashed some severe emotion with the picture she'd taken, and she'd not known how to collar it back up without admitting she'd fudged the truth.

"I took off in my car. It was a foolish thing to do considering my rage, and the beer I'd been drinking." He paused and took a breath. "I couldn't stop in time when a little girl in a stroller pushed by her grandmother crossed the street in front of me. I tried to miss her, but . . . the booze, my inexperience . . . I yanked the steering wheel. It didn't help. I hit her and then spun out into the side of a building."

"Oh, God, that's awful. Sarah."

"Yeah. Sometimes, I can still hear the thud and her grandmother screaming, cursing me to hell. The air bag deployed, the car was a wreck, but I walked away."

Adair wanted to touch him, comfort him, but she didn't move.

"The ambulance came, the police. I was charged. Ironically, a plane crashed into the Atlantic that same day and the news focused on that, so I didn't even make local news."

"That's why you went to juvenile detention."

"Yes."

"I guess that explains why Sarah's mom gave me a free ticket to the race. She set the whole thing up?"

"You figured out it was Lydia?"

"Yes." She looked away for a moment, not wanting to admit to what she'd done. "I found Sarah." No more secrets. She took a deep breath and told him the story.

"God, woman, you're bold. I love that, by the way, and after the way I left you at the race, I don't blame you for wanting answers. Lydia gave me the ticket, too. She was on the organizing committee and had us paired together. I talked to her about it. Her mother gives her a hard time, keeps the bitterness and blame going. I'm not excusing what she did, but if it gives you any solace, she's torturing herself more than anyone else."

"None of it would have happened if I'd not tried to break up you and Carly. I thought she didn't deserve you."

"She didn't."

Adair smiled at that. At least he'd realized how Carly had used him.

"She deserved much better than me."

She gave a soft snort. "I don't think so, Josh. Carly was a pretty superficial person. She was using you."

"Adair, I wasn't angry at Carly because she thought I'd cheated. I was angry because I thought her aunt was my ticket into a graphic arts program. She was head of the department and the competition to get into that program was fierce. Carly planned to tell her aunt I'd humiliated her. I knew there was no love between us."

Carly had never mentioned the connection to her aunt.

"What happened to Sarah wasn't your fault, Adair. I don't want you to feel responsible. I've done enough of that for both of us."

Adair quietly absorbed everything Josh said.

"Josh, I'm really sorry for all of it. I was—"

"Stop, don't say another sorry, not another word about it. It's long over."

"You're right. And because I've promised myself no more secrets, I have one more admission. At the beginning of the race, I didn't hear all the rules, so I never knew what the elimination challenge was. What was it? It must have been horrible."

He grimaced. "Yeah, it was. I really can't dance."

"Dance. Are you serious? That was it?"

"Damn right I'm serious—a solo salsa routine. Do you have any idea how humiliating that would have been?"

She laughed. "Good grief, you can't be that bad."

"Trust me, I can." He kissed her cut finger, then looked into her eyes. "Adair, would you consider a dinner date with me, one without a race to the finish?"

"As soon as this show is over, yes, I would." Her heart took up more space in her chest, like it was fueled by both release and possibility. She remembered something Annalise from the full circle group said: *If you don't let go of the guilt, nothing good can fill that space.*

"Actually, on second thought, I have to eat dinner tonight if you're free."

"For you, I am." His smile freed the earth from spinning on its axis. "One more thing we need to do before I help you empty these boxes." His hands slid down her sides to sit on her hips igniting a desire to buy new lacy lingerie, perfumed oils and scented candles. Their lips met in a kiss, soft yet intense.

They didn't need any more words. Race of Hearts had given their romance a heartbeat and now all they needed was time to restart their beginning—time, forgiveness and a good bottle of wine.

And one more thing, she thought, as he pressed a little closer.

A pair of fuzzy, pink handcuffs.

was time to restart their beginning—time, forgiveness and a good bottle of wine.

And one more thing, she thought, as he pressed a little closer.

A pair of fuzzy, pink handcuffs.

ACKNOWLEDGMENTS

As always, I couldn't do this without my beta readers and critique group: Carole-Ann Vance, Linda Farmer, Jennifer Filipowicz, Irene Jorgensen and Urve Tamburg, and a special shout-out to my critique partner extraordinaire, Sherry Isaac! Thank you all for the time it takes to give a constructive critique.

I want to thank my editor for strengthening this story and for her copy-editing skills.

I also want to thank two incredible women who helped me get facts straight (at least I hope I did), Susan Mann, holistic energy healer and Martha McGuire, M.S.W., among other momentous credentials and achievements.

Dear Reader,

Thank you for taking time to read *Race of Hearts*. If you enjoyed it, please consider telling your friends, or posting an honest review. Word of mouth is an author's best friend and much appreciated.

May you always have love in your life.

Sharon Clare

Get your FREE book by signing up for my email list on my website at www.sharonclare.com and receive updates on the next book in the Full Circle Series – *Clash of Hearts*!

ABOUT THE AUTHOR

Life has enough difficult times, so it's important to me to write novels where happiness ultimately triumphs. I help my characters overcome their demons, open their hearts, and find the love everyone deserves.

When you reach the end, I strive to leave you in a happy place.

Learn about the Magical Matchmaker Series by visiting my website at: www.sharonclare.com

I'd love to connect with you on:

Facebook: www.facebook.com/sclarewriter/

Twitter: @sclarewriter

Made in the USA
Columbia, SC
20 September 2017